Teenagers from Mars

By M. Bray

Teenagers from Mars

Copyright © 2022 by M. Bray

ISBN 9798788531441

Side *One*

Track 1: Sunday Morning

September, 1987

On July 1, 1979, Sony introduced the first ever portable cassette player. It was a fourteen-ounce blue-and-silver hunk of plastic with two clunky buttons, headphones, and a leather case. I found one at a Salvation Army for a dollar back in '83, but by that point, the leather case was long gone, the plastic was total crap, and if you wanted to rewind your tape, you had to do it with a pencil. The thing was completely busted, but it didn't really matter; that Walkman was totally boss.

That was of course until my father went mental and smashed it with the heel of his steel toe boot. Now, it was probably laying wasted in some junk yard, shattered into a million pieces. The only thing I had left was a single, pathetic cassette tape. That particular morning, I messed with it in my pocket as I sat on a bench outside the Midtowne train station and waited for my aunt to pick me up.

In front of me, the guy who worked the ticket booth held a menthol cigarette between his fingers while he watched an episode of Alf on a busted old television. Every few minutes, he'd take a puff and let out a hoarse laugh. God, I wished I could laugh like that, but that wasn't going to happen any time soon; I was just too damn nervous. At any moment, I was supposed to meet my total-stranger-of-an-aunt for the first time ever. I had no clue what she even looked like, and now I was supposed to go *live* with her. With each train that came and went, a whole new herd of strangers swarmed the station. Any one of those people could've been her; the thought was enough to send my stomach to my knees.

I yanked out my cassette tape and ran my fingers over the plastic cover. *Born to Run* by the Boss himself, Bruce Springsteen. It was one of my all-time favorite albums. I'd spent countless hours staring at that black and white cover, not to mention I'd read and reread the track listing just about a zillion times. *Thunder Road* was my favorite of course, but *Tenth Avenue Freeze-Out* was also pretty heavy. And I definitely couldn't forget about *Backstreets* or *Jungleland.* Come to think of it, they were all pretty much my favorite.

After a while my nerves eased and I imagined Bruce's raspy voice in the back of my mind. I didn't need a cassette player; that song was forever ingrained into my memory. When things got bad, I'd just close my eyes and remember the words. It was my trick. An escape from my crappy reality. That was the beauty of music—it was the one thing my father couldn't take from me.

Just as I started to fully lose myself, my name was shouted from across the station. I looked up to see a woman booking it through the crowd like a frickin' linebacker. She wore high-waisted denim jeans, plum lipstick, and a long flowing zebra print cardigan with shoulder pads. As she got closer, it became pretty obvious that those weren't shoulder pads—her arms were *ginormous.* And she had to be at least six feet tall. When she finally stopped in front of me, she was out of breath.

"I'm looking for my nephew," she said. "Charlie Stewart?"

I had barely even nodded when she yanked me to my feet and pulled me into a tight bear hug.

"It's me," she said. "Your Aunt Joy. I'm so sorry I'm late."

She rocked me back and forth as I held my breath, drowning in a wave of auburn hair and floral perfume. When she finally pulled away, she grabbed my shoulders tight and looked me over with a grin.

"Gosh," she said. "You look just like your father when he was seventeen."

It was like a punch to the gut. *My father.* God, the last person I ever wanted to think about was my father. The only thing I had in common with that man was our curly brown hair. We didn't even have the same colored eyes. His were blue and mine were green. I must've done a bad job at hiding my disgust because my aunt's eyes shot open and her gaze trailed to the stitches on my left cheekbone. They were totally gnarly—woven only days prior, the gash still fresh in my skin.

"I'm so sorry," she said.

"It's fine," I mumbled, my face burning red as I looked away.

There was a painfully long and awkward silence until she let out a short laugh. "What a great way to start, huh?" She grabbed my bag of clothes and swung it over her shoulder. "Come on, let's get you home. You must be exhausted."

I trudged along in her footsteps until we stopped in front of a light blue Toyota Cressida with a faded Mondale and Ferraro '84 bumper sticker peeling on the back. As she tossed my bag in the trunk, I slid into the passenger's seat and pretty much just gawked at the dashboard, trying to comprehend the situation.

Here I was, about to move in with a woman I'd never met before. What if she hated me? Or what if she was just as mental as my father? Thankfully she wasn't related to him by blood since she was my mother's sister and all, but still, I'd never met my mother. She died giving birth to me, so for all I knew, she could've been just as insane. I mean, hell. She had to be if she was with someone like my father, right? My mind continued racing until I thought I was going to yak, which was pretty typical for me. I was about as shy as they come and had anxiety through the roof. In fact, it wasn't until Aunt Joy started the car and music erupted from the speakers that I snapped out of it.

"Sorry about that," she said as she turned down the volume. "I'm a sucker for Madonna. Are you a fan?"

I pressed my lips together and shrugged.

"You don't know?" she asked.

"Not really," I said.

"Oh come on, Charlie, how can you not like Madonna?"

She threw her head back and began to sing with the most obnoxious falsetto I'd ever heard. She fanned her sparkling red fingernails over her face while singing into a fake microphone. I stared in shock until she finally stopped, her hand draped over her forehead as if she had just performed for an entire stadium.

As lame as it was, I couldn't help but smile.

"Ha! I knew I could get you to warm up." She placed her keys in the ignition and backed the car out. "So, you a big Springsteen fan?"

I frowned. "Yeah, how'd you know?"

"I saw your cassette tape. If you'd like, we could give it a listen instead of this ol' Madonna mix."

"No, that's okay."

"You sure?"

I nodded.

She glanced at me and smiled. "Well then, I hope you don't mind me singing."

We continued along a two lane highway, the silence starting to grow unbearable. I looked out the window and tried to get an idea of what Midtowne might be like. It seemed boring enough with way too many trees and old shops that had either gone out of business or were on their way out.

"So Charlie," my aunt said, finally, "are you excited about your new school?"

I slumped in my seat and sighed. A new school wasn't all that new to me. Every few months, dear ol' Dad would get paranoid about something or another, turn into a total spaz, and force us to uproot our trailer. And with each move, it never got easier. A new school meant new people and new problems, and forget about making friends. After a while, I just sort of gave up.

"I guess," I mumbled.

"Oh, honey," she said, "I know new schools are hard, but I promise you're going to love it. Midtowne's a bit on the small side, but D.C. is just a short train ride away, so there's plenty to do. And I hear…"

Her voice droned on and on, so I kind of just left her to it. It was clear she was more than happy to lead the conversation and I had no interest in talking, so it was a great match. She must've been going on nonstop for close to fifteen minutes when she finally nudged me with her elbow.

"So tell me, Charlie," she said. "What do you do for—"

A siren whizzed past our car. It was as if someone fired a gun off right in front of my face and a rush of adrenaline coursed through me. I sat bolt upright, watching as a bright red fire truck barreled down the empty road, its red and blue lights flickering like a strobe. I stared after the truck until it disappeared over the horizon. Even though it was gone, I could still hear the siren blaring in my head.

"You there?" she asked.

"Huh?"

She let out a soft laugh. "I asked what you do for fun."

I forced myself to forget about the firetruck and eased back in my seat. What *did* I do for fun? Well, I spent most of my time avoiding home, so I racked up a ton of hours at the library. That, and I was big on hitting up local music stores so I could sponge off their second-hand instruments. It was pretty pathetic, but at least it was something.

"I like music," I said.

"That's lovely. Do you play any instruments?"

"Guitar."

Her eyebrows raised. "Oh, that's—"

Another firetruck zoomed past us. I hardly had time to process it when two police cars followed right behind, moving like lightning down the empty highway. It was then I noticed a thick cloud of smoke rising above a line of trees; it couldn't have been more than a few miles away. As soon as Aunt Joy saw it, she gasped and slammed her foot on the accelerator. With each passing second the smoke grew darker and thicker until finally we pulled up to a road block. Aunt Joy wasted no time in turning off the car and getting out.

"Wait here," she said, as she closed the door behind her.

I leaned forward, my hands resting on the dashboard. There were ten or so police trying to form a barrier as a small crowd pointed to a building in the forest clearing, whispering as firemen did their best to extinguish the flames. It was totally wild and from what I could tell, it looked like a small theatre, or at least what was left of one. The entire top half was pretty much gone, nothing more than steel beams and framework in the vague shape of a stage. The remaining brick walls were blackened by soot and surrounded by piles of ash.

I got out of the car, and as soon as I stood, a wave of heat swelled in the air causing my upper lip to sweat. I held my breath as I watched the firefighters shouting over the sound of sirens and crackling flames. Sure it was tragic, but it was also captivating. I'd never seen a fire up close, but let me tell you, it was pretty heavy. Just totally unreal. And I was even more mesmerized when they brought out the hose. It was the sort of thing you heard about on the news, but when you physically saw it right in front of you, it was something else. I watched in awe for at least half an hour until the final flames were vanquished and the crowd began to thin out.

Just then, there was a hard elbow to my ribs as some kid shoved past me. I came back to reality and stared after him with my eyebrow arched, but he didn't even seem to notice me. He strutted right up to a police officer and began firing off questions as if he were the top detective on the case. He looked to be about my age, with long brown hair tucked under a rolled up red bandanna. Even more odd, he wore a long trench coat, army pants, and boots despite it being a scorching August day in Virginia. After giving the cop the third degree, he began inspecting a wooden sign. It was small and seemed relatively unscathed by the flames and read *Midtowne Community Theatre* in gold lettering. He ran his fingers over every last inch before scribbling something in his notebook.

A sudden hand on my shoulder stole my attention. I turned back to find Aunt Joy standing next to me with tears in her eyes.

"I'm so sorry you had to see this, Charlie," she said. "Gosh, I just hope no one was inside."

I let out a deep sigh and looked back to the grisly scene. Of course I also hoped no one was inside, but the longer I stared at the crumbled remains of the theatre, the more I knew that just wasn't true.

When I saw the first spirit rise from the ashes, I wanted to look away, but I knew it wouldn't change the fact that he was dead. His skin was melted to the bone and completely covered in soot. He had patchy brown hair, though I wasn't sure if it was actually brown or just dirty, and wore what looked like a pirate costume, complete with a black eye patch and a goofy fake parrot on his shoulder. Soon after, more spirits arose from the dirt. One after the other, they appeared as if they'd been birthed from the ground. There had to be at least twenty, all with different costumes—there was a younger woman with a short pixie cut that was dressed in green tights; two nearly identical men with powdered wigs and long brown overcoats; a bunch more pirates with fake swords and peg legs. All of them had the same yellowing eyes and skin that glowed like embers. And I could smell it—an acrid scent I'd never forget. They walked with a limp, inching toward me as if they knew I could see them.

Aunt Joy said something, but I tuned her out. Besides, I knew she couldn't see them. I'm glad she couldn't; I'd never wish that burden on anyone.

I locked eyes with a little girl, the ends of her curled blonde pigtails singed. Her eyes were cold, empty pits that went on for an eternity. She wore a pink nightgown that was almost completely charred and stained brown. It was then that it hit me. Wendy. Yeah, that had to be it. All the pirates and the green tights—the theatre must've been doing a production of Peter Pan. The little girl had one of those porcelain dolls with a matching dress, though it's face was cracked and melted into a grotesque shape, leaving it looking like it came straight out of Chernobyl.

The sad thing was, she couldn't have been older than eleven.

Aunt Joy seemed nice enough, though kind of strange at times. This was made especially clear when I first got to see the inside of her house. On the outside it sure seemed normal enough—modest in size, fresh cut lawn, and to top it all off there was even a porch swing. It was exactly what I imagined a cookie cutter suburban home would look like. But as soon as I walked inside, my jaw dropped to the floor.

Her living room walls were totally dedicated to old records and neon silkscreen prints that ranged from celebrity portraits all the way to pictures of nude body parts and cans of tomato soup. There was a bunny ears television resting on top of an antique armoire that was turned on low and stationed to a Boy George music video on MTV. Her couch was buried beneath fluffy pillows of all different colors and sequined blankets. It seemed like everything had to be over the top, gold trim, cheetah print, and glitter. There was even a large stone sculpture of a naked woman that had a pink, feathery boa draped around its neck. I'd be lying if I said I didn't blush when I saw that.

That evening, she cooked dinner which was served on a nice pink and gold china set. Now, I'd never had chicken pot pie before, and I'm sure it was great, but I was way too nauseous to eat anything. Instead, I pushed the food around while my aunt hurled non-stop questions at me.

"Oh, I'm just so glad you're here," she said for the umpteenth time. She took a bite of food before nodding to my plate. "You haven't touched your dinner, sweetheart. Do you not like it?"

"No, it's fine."

"How would you know if you haven't even taken a bite?"

"Sorry," I said. "I'm just not hungry."

She placed her fork on the table and sighed. "That's okay, honey. I understand. It's been a long day. I'm sure you just want to unpack your things and get settled in your room."

There was nothing I wanted more.

She grabbed her napkin and dabbed her mouth. "Listen, Charlie, before you go, there's a few things I wanted to go over. First of all, I want you to feel at home. That's very important to me, okay?"

"Okay," I said.

"Good. Now, the fridge is always stocked, so whenever you're hungry, please help yourself. I'd hate for you to feel uncomfortable eating in your own home. Do you have any favorite foods you want me to pick up from the store?"

I shrugged.

"Oh come on, there has to be something you like."

To me, food was food. If it was there, I ate it; it was as simple as that. But it sounded like she wasn't going to give up anytime soon, so I said the first thing that came to mind.

"Apples," I said.

"Apples?"

"Yeah…" I looked at my plate, my face burning red. "Apples would be great."

She let out a soft laugh. "I can manage that. Anything else?"

I shook my head.

"Right, well apples it is," she said. "One last thing. I work in the city most nights, so you'll have the place to yourself. I understand you're almost an adult now, so I don't really see much use in enforcing a ton of rules. I trust you. The only thing I ask is to not go in my room. Just as your room is your private space, that's mine, okay?"

I found it kind of odd that *that* was where she drew the line. I mean, she had naked statues all over her place for crying out loud. I couldn't even begin to imagine what else she could be hiding. But I didn't really press her considering I just wanted to be alone, so I simply nodded.

"Good," she said.

After we cleaned our dishes, she walked me to my room. I held my breath and wondered what sort of whacky furnishings I'd find there. I wasn't sure I'd be able to sleep if the walls were neon or the pillows were made of cheetah fur. But when the door opened, and I saw it was just a simple bed, dresser, mirror, and closet, I almost collapsed in relief. Of course there was the small statue of a butt-ass-naked man sitting atop the dresser, but I figured that'd be easy to stash in a drawer the second Aunt Joy left.

"Bathroom's down the hall," she said. "Those blankets should be enough, but if you find yourself cold in the middle of the night, there's more in the closet. My room is just next door, so if you need anything, just knock."

I nodded.

She smiled and grabbed the knob. "All right then, honey. Sweet dreams."

The second she closed the door, a deafening silence filled the room. It was the type that was so loud, your ears started to ring. I began to walk around the empty space, not sure what to do with myself. I thought being alone was what I wanted, but there was something totally eerie about it. It made everything so much more real. This was home now. No more trailer park. No more Dad. Through gritted teeth, I pushed the memories from my mind as I grabbed the trash bag that I had packed and dumped my pitiful collection of raggy clothes and old trinkets on the bed. This included a few wooden stakes, a bottle of wolf's bane, and an old sapphire amulet that was supposed to ward off demons—you know, normal teenage stuff.

The shirt I wore reeked of smoke from the fire earlier, so I was desperate to change it. The last thing I wanted to think about was the image of that little girl's ghost. I peeled my shirt off, and as I did, my reflection in the mirror caught my eye. Barf me out; I hated my body. As much as I wanted to look away, I couldn't. It was a tractor beam pulling me in.

I'd always been a relatively skinny kid, but that wasn't what made me want to hurl. It was the cigar burns that dotted across my chest and resembled a cluster of stars; the football-sized bruise on my side that was now a disturbing shade of purple and yellow; the random scars across my torso. But even through all that, the one thing I couldn't take my eyes off of was the fresh gash in my side. It was thick, roughly six inches in length and held together by stitches just like the ones on my cheek. The longer I stared, the more panicked I felt until it became hard to breathe. I quickly forced myself to look away, snatched the closest shirt, and threw it over my head.

I sprawled on my bed, but the thought kept pestering me. I rubbed my hands over my face, forcing in deep breaths. It didn't help. Nothing did. I just couldn't shake the memory. It was all so clear—the sound of a record scratching; the smell of my father's cheap Irish whiskey; the intense heat as the shard of glass dug deep into my side. I rolled over and buried my head in a pillow. I just wanted some peace and quiet, but that stupid song kept scratching at the back of my head. *Come Softly To Me* by the Fleetwoods. God, I hated that song. I hated it so damn much.

Before I knew it, I was back in the trailer. My father was screaming over the music as he paced back and forth, ranting and raving just like he always did. I was tucked in the back of the closet, my head in my hands as I tried to think of something else. *Anything* else. I hated when he was like this.

No.

I couldn't be in the trailer. I was in Midtowne. I lived with Aunt Joy now. I was safe. But his voice was so clear, it just had to be real. *Radar. Radar. Charlie, he's coming!*

In a sudden burst of adrenaline, I shot to my feet and headed straight for the closet. As I slammed the door behind me, I crumpled up in a ball and started pinching and scratching at my legs. After a while, my breathing slowed as I rocked back and forth. He wasn't here. I was in Midtowne. I lived with Aunt Joy now.

I was safe.

I was safe.

Safe.

I repeated that over and over until my nerves eased.

When I finally caught my breath, I closed my eyes and cursed myself. The closet. That damn closet. I had to be screwed in the head to find comfort in the one place I hated most.

***

When my alarm went off the next morning, it was oddly dark. I blinked a few times, confused until I glanced out the window to find the sun totally blocked by a thick cluster of clouds. The sky had a yellowish tint to it that made it seem like a storm might be coming. I should've seen it as some sort of omen and went back to sleep, but instead, I rolled out of bed like a total idiot and went to school.

You'd think I'd get used to the first day of school considering I moved so much, but it never ceased to amaze me just how draining it could be. The school itself was nothing special. In fact, it was shockingly similar to every other high school I'd ever been to. You know the type—dented lockers with third-rate combination locks; hallways jam-packed with way too many people; those tacky PSA flyers begging kids not to do drugs pinned on every last bulletin board. And no matter where I went, everyone seemed to dress like they were straight out of the latest John Hughes movie. I wished I could go the rest of my life without having to see another pair of Reebok high tops or acid washed jeans. I was never one for fashion and often wore my father's dirty old flannels and a pair of beaten up Keds which did me no favors in terms of fitting in.

Classes were okay, aside from the teachers that made me stand up and introduce myself; that was hell. I also caught a few elbows in the hallway and got my books knocked out of my hands, but as the new kid, that was expected. At least I was able to sneak away to the library at lunch. It was decent in size and had a totally awesome selection of older books with tons of private tables and places to sit. I found a book about ancient Egyptian mummies with pages that were so covered in dust, I figured it hadn't been read for at least a decade. Overall, my day was a total yawn-fest until last period chemistry rolled around and I met my lab partner.

As soon as I saw him, my mouth went dry and continued to get drier as he bounced toward me—and when I said bounced, I meant *bounced*. It was as if he were dancing to some imaginary tune only he could hear. He was about my height, though he was stockier with shaggy blond hair that fell past his ears. Instead of acid washed jeans, his were ripped and black and covered in chains and spikes. On top of that, he wore a t-shirt depicting a creepy amphibian *thing* lurking in a sewer with the word C.H.U.D. written above it. When he finally got to my table, he took the stool next to me and threw his backpack down which was torn to shreds and covered in patches and safety pins. I caught a glimpse of some of those patches—something about anarchy in the U.K. and another warning Nazi Punks to fuck off, whatever that meant. Before I could say a word, he snatched my hand and violently shook it.

"Looks like we're lab partners," he said. "The name's Mick. And before you say it, I was *not* named after Mick Jagger from the Stones. Screw the Stones, man. I'm more of a Mick Jones from the Clash type of guy. Too bad none of the lame-oid preppies at this school even know who that is. All they listen to is that generic new wave garbage like Duran Duran or Genesis. Man, I hate Genesis. Phil Collins can kiss my ass. Anyway, what's your name?"

He spoke so fast, his words blurred together. In fact, it took me a solid minute to even realize he'd asked me a question. I quickly straightened and cleared my throat.

"Charlie," I said.

"Charlie, eh? That's a radical name, man. I dig it. Kind of like that singer from the UK Subs, Charlie Harper or whatever. Or you know that song, Charlie Don't Surf. Damn, that's a good one. You know it?"

I wasn't sure what else to do, so I merely shrugged.

He laughed and shook his head. "Yeah, you're right, man. Screw the Clash. I'm much more into the hardcore scene. You know, like Bad Brains and Minor Threat. How about you, man, you dig punk?"

I had no idea what that meant, but luckily the teacher interrupted and called for the class to quiet down. I sighed in relief and grabbed a pencil and paper from my backpack.

Mick leaned to my ear and whispered, "We'll talk more later."

God, I hoped not.

I found it hard to focus after that, and not just because he spent the entire class period humming and drawing on his hands and arms to the point that they were totally covered in sharpie marker. No. As strange as all that was, I couldn't stop staring for a different reason. From the moment he walked into the room, I could smell the familiar amber and almond scent. Every few seconds a faint crimson glow wafted from his skin. And then there was my gut screaming at me whenever I laid my eyes on him. I just couldn't ignore it.

He was a damn werewolf.

Let me preface this by saying I was fully aware that seeing ghosts and werewolves wasn't normal. I mean, it wasn't like I *wanted* to see them, I just sort of did. And it wasn't just ghosts and werewolves either. From the very little I understood, there were hundreds, maybe even thousands of different creatures and species out there, some disguised as humans, some not, but for whatever the hell reason, I was able to see them. The only other person I knew who could do this was my father, though I wasn't sure that was a good thing considering the guy was a total nut job.

I moved my stool as far from Mick as possible but still watched him from the corner of my eye. He was like an excited puppy. A total ball of energy, constantly drumming on his desk and singing under his breath. At one point, the teacher even had to stop class to tell him to knock it off.

"My bad," Mick said, holding up his hand.

The teacher rolled his eyes and turned back to the board as if this wasn't the first time it happened.

After keeping an eye on Mick the entire class period, I came to the conclusion that the dude seemed harmless enough, though I still figured it'd be in my best interest to carry around some of that wolf's bane I had luckily thought to pack. It was only a small amount, but I figured it'd do the trick in case I ever needed it.

As soon as the final bell rang, I snatched my things and booked it out of class before Mick had a chance to talk to me again. I kept checking over my shoulder until I was out of the building and on the walk home, and even then, I glanced back here and there.

For the most part, Midtowne seemed pretty lame aside from the whole werewolf situation. It was your typical small town with old brick buildings and plenty of parks. It was divided in half by a set of train tracks, and right smack dab in the center was a diner with a sign that read *World's Greatest Pie*—not sure how much more cliché you could get than that. The only thing that wasn't picture perfect was the weather. Just as it had been that morning, the sky was dark and gloomy. It definitely looked like rain.

As I turned the street corner in front of a cafe that promised bottomless cups of coffee, something peculiar caught my eye. I stopped dead in my tracks, my brow scrunching together as I looked it over. At first, I thought I was imagining things; I had to be. But the longer I stared, the tighter my chest grew.

It was the little girl from the fire.

The rest of the world faded, and our eyes were locked as if we were the only two beings in existence. She had the same lifeless stare as before, her skin blistered and covered in pus. She even had that same creepy doll. It dangled at her side, broken and melted. I must've been standing there for a solid minute when I heard a voice.

"What're you staring at?"

I spun around, surprised to find the guy from the fire standing before me. The one that had shoved past me and was scribbling in his notebook. He even had on the same trench coat and rolled-up red bandanna tied over his forehead.

"Excuse me?" I asked.

"I wanted to know what you were staring at," he said again.

Before I could fully process his question, he lifted his finger and pointed to the street corner. It was then that I noticed the ghost had vanished. I perked up and began scouring the nearby streets, but she was nowhere to be found.

"You see something, don't you?" he asked.

"No," I said quickly.

He narrowed his eyes and looked me over. "Right… Well anyway, my name's Scotty Beauchamp. Pleasure to meet you."

"Charlie," I replied.

He repeated my name, stretching out every last syllable. It might've been his forward approach or the way his eyes seared with intensity, but something didn't feel right. It was as if he could see right through to the deepest depths of my soul. I had the sudden urge to get out of there, so I muttered some stupid excuse and jetted off without looking back.

When I got home, I locked the door behind me and collapsed at the kitchen table. As I buried my head in my hands, I began to wonder who this kid was and what exactly he knew about me. Not only that, but I wondered how the hell he knew there was something on that street corner. After a while, I gritted my teeth and pushed those thoughts from my mind. I decided right then and there that I was going to be normal. The whole weird, freaky kid with the supernatural visions was officially behind me. No more dad. No more trailer. No more damn ghosts. I was normal.

Normal.

As I stared at the table, my stomach twisted. It didn't matter how many times I repeated it; I knew deep down it would never be true.

By the time Friday rolled around, I was totally pumped for the weekend; I had grand plans to hide in my room for two days straight and not talk to anyone. But I wasn't home safe just yet; I had to get through last period chemistry, and that meant dealing with Mick. Every single day, he'd strut in the room wearing a different t-shirt, each more ridiculous than the last. One day, it was a guy with a strange green liquid oozing out of his mouth and eyes. *The Stuff* it said in big purple letters. I figured it was a movie or something. Another shirt had a killer tomato with a face and monstrous fangs. And all throughout the class period, he'd chat my ear off about Jello Biafra this or Ian Mackaye that. That week I learned more about east and west coast punk than I did chemistry.

When the last bell for the day finally rang, I was ready to get the hell out of there. Mick was mid-sentence when I pushed out my chair and stood, but before I could grab my backpack, someone shoved past me and knocked it to the floor. I watched in defeat as my pencils and papers spilled everywhere.

"Sorry," the kid said, though there was no hiding his shit-eating grin. "Didn't see you there."

"It's okay," I mumbled.

He joined his friends at the front of the room as they high-fived and laughed. By that point in the week, I was pretty used to getting my crap knocked to the ground, so I ignored them and began shoving my things back into my bag.

"Those guys are assholes," Mick said, squatting next to me.

I stopped and watched as he began to collect my things. With every move he made, his deep red aura drifted from his skin like smoke, and his amber scent grew even stronger. I glanced over my shoulder as the room began to thin out; the last thing I wanted was to be alone with a werewolf.

"You don't have to do that," I said quickly.

"Nah, man, don't worry about it."

"Really, I just—"

"I don't mind, seriously." He handed me the bag of Cheez Balls Aunt Joy had packed for me and smirked. "You know, my mom used to buy these for me when I was younger. I ate them so much she started getting that massive plastic container they sell at Wegmans. Too bad I chomped through that in about a week. She'd get so pissed."

"Yeah," I said, forcing a laugh.

"I also dig Fruit Wrinkles. I can eat that shit all day, man. They're this new thing, sort of like Fruit Roll-ups, but better. My friends think they're beyond nasty, but they're dead wrong. You ever try 'em before?"

I shook my head.

He nudged my arm and grinned. "That's tragic, man. I'll have to bring a pack for you on Monday."

I reached beneath our lab table to fish out one of my pens, but just as I wrapped my fingers around it, Mick yelped and shot to his feet. I immediately dropped the pen and whipped around, my heart skipping a beat once I caught sight of the terrified look on his face.

"What?" I asked.

"Why do you have that?"

"Have what?"

He raised a shaky hand and pointed to the floor. "*That.*"

It was then that I noticed my bottle of wolf's bane peeking from beneath a notebook. Its glass shell had cracked open and the earthy scent was just starting to fill the room. It was like a weight dropped onto my chest. With each passing second, my heart beat louder and louder until I was sure he could hear it. The wolf's bane. God, I was a moron. I totally forgot I had it in my bag.

"Charlie," Mick said softly.

I looked up to find him wide-eyed. He was clearly waiting for me to say something, only there was nothing. No words that could possibly explain why the hell I was carrying around wolf's bane—well, other than the truth, but there was no way in hell I was telling him that. After a moment, I cleared my throat.

"It's nothing," I said.

"Nothing?"

"Yeah, it's just…" I rubbed the back of my neck. "My aunt. She has this thing for exotic foliage and asked me to pick this up for her the other day. I guess I just forgot it was there, you know?"

He raised his eyebrow. "Exotic *foliage*?"

I forced a smile and nodded, but it was obvious he knew I was full of crap. Before he could say another word, I gathered the rest of my things.

"I should get going," I said.

I booked it past him and continued down the hallway, not even stopping at my locker. When I was finally outside, my face burned red as I replayed our conversation over and over. The way I tripped over my words and rambled on and on about exotic plants—the guy probably thought I was totally Looney Toons.

My mind continued racing until I finally got home and collapsed against the front door. I pressed my hand to my forehead and reminded myself I had two days to think up a plan. Two whole days. And who knows? Maybe I was just being paranoid. Hell, maybe he bought the whole exotic foliage crap. Things might be all right, so long as I quit acting like a total spazoid.

Right.

I was finally able to get a grip after a few deep breaths and glanced at the television which was mindlessly playing a rerun of Happy Days. It was that one where the redhead doesn't let the Fonz cheat on a test because it wasn't the *right* thing to do. I never saw the end to that one but assumed it was the same ol' hunky dory, feel-good ending most sitcoms had. *Barf.* I rolled my eyes and switched it off before heading to the kitchen. I expected to find Aunt Joy sipping her New York Seltzer flavored soda like she always was, but today she was nowhere to be found. In fact, the only thing there was a small box and a handwritten note next to it.

It was wrapped with sparkling purple paper and complete with a golden glitter ribbon; obviously it was from Aunt Joy. I grabbed the piece of paper and brought it close, recognizing the loopy handwriting to be hers.

Charlie,

I really wanted to give you this in person, but I had to head to work early tonight. Promise we'll do something special this weekend, just the two of us. Until then, enjoy this present. I love you, honey.

-Aunt Joy

I lowered it and frowned. She got me a present. A *present.* But why? I guess my birthday was only a week away, but even so, I'd never gotten a birthday present before, so it wasn't like I expected anything.

And she definitely didn't owe me. If anything, I owed *her*. It wasn't right for me to accept this. Then again, if I didn't open it, I would look like an ungrateful ass. I must've gone back and forth for at least five minutes before deciding to just be normal for once and open the damn thing.

I reluctantly picked up the gift and began unwrapping the paper, careful not to tear it. Knowing Aunt Joy, she'd probably knit me a hat or something. My guess was that it was big and purple, or maybe even cheetah print. That, or she bought me some outlandish mittens or boots. She was always going on and on about how I barely had any clothes and wouldn't survive the winter. But no matter what it was, I'd wear it for her, especially since she went through all the trouble. But when I finally got it open, my heart skipped a beat. It wasn't a hat or mittens or even new boots.

It was a Walkman.

I stared at it, a breath caught in my lungs. A *Walkman*. She must've seen me messing around with that frickin' Springsteen cassette and felt bad for me. Yeah, that had to be it; she felt bad. I began running my fingers over the box. It was sleek and black with no scuffs or cracks in the plastic, clearly much nicer than my old one. I laid it back on the table and grabbed the note, but no matter how many times I read it, I just couldn't figure out why she got this for me. I mean, she barely even knew me.

I glossed over her words again and again, getting caught up on the last line each time. I forced myself to read it until a lump grew in my throat. It was then that it hit me.

I love you, honey.

No one had ever said that to me before.

The next morning, I watched the news over a bowl of Cheerios. To be honest, I was never really one for the local news, but the story they were covering had me absolutely enamored.

Apparently, Midtowne had seen a rise in suicides the past couple of days. Totally gnarly ones, too. Like, apparently, some guy had been shopping at the local Home Depot when out of nowhere, he got a sudden hankering for some Drano. The guy's brother said he'd made a dart for the plumbing aisle and was about half a bottle deep before he could stop him. Another lady decided to take an afternoon stroll across a busy four lane highway. She didn't even make it more than ten steps before getting clipped by a semi-truck. One story after the other, all of them the same. A totally normal person just living their lives like normal and then *BAM*! They off themselves. I will admit, the story was totally morbid, but I couldn't look away. They were just about to report on the names when the TV went black.

"How depressing," Aunt Joy said as she set the remote back on the living room table. She lowered herself next to me and sighed. "You really don't need that right now; you've been through enough."

"Right," I said as I stared at the remote.

The truth was, I wanted nothing more than to snatch it and turn the TV right back on. As much as I was completely absorbed in that story, I also couldn't stop thinking about facing Mick later that day. At least the depressing suicide sagas provided a distraction and let me focus on other people's problems.

She checked her watch. "You'd better get going or else you'll be late. Did you want a ride?"

"I'll be okay."

"Are you sure? It looks like it might rain."

"Yeah, I'm sure. Thanks though."

I gave her a hug goodbye, and as soon as I stepped outside, I realized she was right; it was damp and chilly and the sun was stuck behind a cluster of thick gray clouds. I dug out my new Walkman from my backpack. Even though I only had one tape, it didn't stop me from listening to it nonstop the entire weekend. The speaker was just too crisp; I'd never heard the Boss's voice so clear. After slipping on the headphones, I started the walk to school just as music faded in.

But just as I turned the corner, the neighbor's car came barreling down their driveway. It screeched to a halt right in front of me. I gasped and stumbled back, yanking the headphones from over my ears.

"Jesus," I muttered.

Just then, the driver's side door popped open and a man came rushing around the car. As soon as I saw his face, my mouth fell open and I backed away. He was tall and lanky, his limbs like spindly branches. But that wasn't what caused my guard to go up. No. It was the old burn scars all along the left side of his face and neck. They were so bad, he was missing patches of hair and his left ear was nothing more than a mound of flesh fused to his head.

"Are you all right?" he asked.

I was at a total loss for words until it finally hit me that he'd asked a question. I forced myself to stop gawking at the poor guy and looked to the ground.

"I'm fine," I mumbled.

"You sure?"

"Yeah."

The tension mounted as I gripped the straps of my bag until my knuckles turned white. You could make out the faint sounds of

Backstreets playing from the headphone that hung around my neck; it made it all the more awkward. Just when I thought I couldn't take it anymore, he laughed and leaned against the car.

"I know what you're thinking," he said.

"You do?"

His lip curled. "Of course. I'm an actor. I get it all the time. You recognize me from my work in the Return of the Jedi, don't you?" He cupped his hand over his mouth and lowered his voice. "*Luke, I am your father.*"

He dropped his hand and looked to me as if he were waiting for a reaction of some kind. Unfortunately, I had no clue what the hell he was on about. After a moment, his eyes grew wide with disbelief.

"Oh come on," he said. "Darth Vader? The bad guy with the burns all over his face? You're telling me you've never seen Star Wars before?"

I shrugged. "Not really."

He ran his fingers through the patchy remains of his hair and laughed. "Wow, I must be getting old."

"Sorry," I said.

"No, it's not your fault. It was a terrible joke. Believe it or not, I'm fully aware that I'm not the most handsome man in the world, so naturally I like to cut the tension with some humor. The only problem is, I'm not all that funny."

My lip twitched. "You're funny."

"Don't do that."

"Do what?"

"Lie to me to make me feel better. I can tell you're a nice young man, but I don't need your pity. I can handle a bit of criticism." He smiled and stuck out his hand. "Anyway, I'm Edgar. I take it you're Charlie?"

"Yeah, how'd you know?" I asked.

"I spoke with your aunt," he said. "I moved in a few weeks ago myself, so it looks like you and I are the new kids on the block." He glanced at his watch. "Anyway, I'll let you get going. It was nice to finally meet you, Charlie. And I'm sorry again for almost running you down."

As he got back in his car and drove off, I stared after him, my eyebrow raised. You know, for someone so badly scarred, he was pretty upbeat. I mean, talk about not judging a book by its cover, right? For a brief moment, I wondered about those burn scars and how he got them, but then my mind begrudgingly drifted back to Mick and the thought of facing him during seventh period chemistry.

Crap.

I glanced over my shoulder at Aunt Joy's place and wondered if it would really be all that bad to play hookey just this once. Of course I knew I'd have to bite the bullet eventually, but it was way too tempting to push it off just one more day—especially when I pictured Mick's razor sharp teeth glowing in the moonlight and tearing me limb from limb. I shuddered and decided right then and there that I would ditch.

I slipped my headphones back on and started down the sidewalk. Since Aunt Joy worked evenings and would be home all day, I decided my best bet was to find a place downtown to chill.

I wandered a bit, popping in and out of random shops. It wasn't long until I found this totally choice second-hand bookstore with vintage oak floors and wooden shelves painted bright shades of teal and yellow. The best part was, it was crammed floor to ceiling with dusty old books. As soon as I walked in, I took a deep breath. God, I loved the smell of old books. I found a beaten up, green couch tucked in the back corner where I knew I wouldn't be bothered and set up shop.

I spent the next few hours bouncing back and forth between catching up on homework and reading for fun. Right around lunch time, I stumbled across a book about ancient European folklore. I was fascinated by this fairy-type creature that was known to steal children right from their beds and replace them with what was called a changeling. Changelings were hard to spot because the differences were so subtle. Maybe their eyes were a smidge further apart or their ears kind of unaligned. It was just enough of a change to make you question your sanity. Sure it was creepy, but I've always loved that sort of thing.

Toward the end of the day, I started to grow restless. All my homework was finished and there was only so much I could read. My eyes began to grow heavy, and it wasn't long until I eventually drifted to sleep. My dream was totally bizarre, too. I remember talking to Edgar, only it wasn't Edgar—it was a changeling. At first, I didn't notice and we were getting along fine. But as the dream went on, it became more and more obvious. For starters, his dark eyes faded to a familiar light blue and his skinny frame filled out. It wasn't until his burn scars started disappearing that I realized he was morphing into my father. I don't exactly remember how it ended, but I do remember waking with a start.

It took a few minutes for reality to settle back in, and when it did, I noticed a girl standing over me. She had long brown hair and was chewing gum like a cow chews grass. Her arms were crossed and she scowled at me as if I'd just kicked her dog or something. I saw a nametag on her apron and realized she probably worked there. I sat up and looked around, still toeing the line between dream and reality.

"What time is it?" I asked.

"Four."

"*Four?*"

"Yeah, that's what I said." She nodded to the mess I'd made and scoffed. "This isn't your living room, you know. You can't sleep here. If you're not gonna buy anything, then why don't you make like a tree and leave?"

"Sorry," I mumbled.

I began to collect my things and quickly put the books away.

It just started to drizzle when I stepped outside, so I pulled up my hood. I figured Aunt Joy was probably on her way to work by that point, so it was safe to go home. Without wasting another second, I pressed play on my Walkman and was just about to set off when a shop down the road caught my eye.

It was called *Blue Dog Records* and was located right next to the train tracks. The cool thing about it was that it had a wall of trippy graffiti on the side of the building as well as a funky black and white striped awning above the front door. It also had signs crammed in the dusty window that advertised records, cassettes, but not only that, second hand instruments. When I read that, my heart skipped a beat and I made an immediate break for it without thinking twice.

As soon as I walked in, my jaw dropped in awe. The first thing that caught my eye was the endless crates of records and cassette tapes all crammed in the center of the store. I noticed some of my all-time favorite albums propped up on a shelf—*Ziggy Stardust and the Spiders from Mar, Lola Versus Power man and the Moneygoround Part One, Rubber Soul, Highway 61 Revisited*—and don't even get me started on the instruments. They seemed to have a little bit of everything, but what really caught my eye were the guitars. There were endless rows of

Fenders, Gibsons, and a beautiful Les Paul hanging with a backlight as if it'd been made by the gods themselves. The body was starburst with a double humbucker which was the same guitar Jimmy Page used.

After finally forcing my mouth shut, I wandered to a room in the back strictly made for acoustic guitars. They were hanging from the walls, on display, and in glass cases. It'd been at least a month since I played, but once I grabbed a Martin acoustic from the rack, I felt right at home. I ran my hands up and down its sleek neck, the wood light and natural with a rosette around the sound hole.

"You play?"

The sudden voice took me by surprise, and I spun around. When I saw it was Mick, I nearly dropped the damn guitar. And just my luck, I was backed in a corner in an empty room with no way out.

"Where were you today?" he asked, taking a step toward me.

"Sick," I said quickly.

"Oh…" He rubbed the back of his neck and shrugged. "Well, you didn't miss much, man. We just went over the periodic table and all those bogus little squares. It was boring as hell, trust me."

He forced a laugh, but it did nothing to cut the tension. In fact, by that point, I was gripping the guitar's neck so tight, I was afraid it might break. I placed it back on the rack and made a move to leave, but before I could, he stepped in front of me.

"So how'd you know?" he asked.

"Know what?"

"Oh, cut the bullshit." He glanced over his shoulder before turning back to me with a lowered voice. "I'm a werewolf, but you already knew that, didn't you?"

I opened my mouth, but no words came out.

"Come on," he pressed. "Just tell me why you had that wolf's bane. What're you like, Van Helsing or something?"

With every word he spoke, he inched closer until I backed into the wall of guitars. One of them fell from its hook and landed with a thud. He stood straight and looked from the guitar to me before letting out a breath.

"I'm sorry," he said. "I'm not mad or anything."

"You're not?"

"No. It's just… no one's ever figured it out before. Then here you come along with your exotic foliage bullshit and you know everything within a week. It just doesn't add up, man. How'd you know? Did I do something to tip you off?"

I shook my head.

"Did I say anything weird?"

"No, it's nothing like that."

"Well then, what is it? Come on, you can tell me."

It became abundantly clear that he wasn't going to give up any time soon. After a moment, I pinched the bridge of my nose and forced out the words.

"I knew from the moment I saw you," I said.

"How?"

"I don't know."

"What do you mean you don't know?"

"I mean I just don't *know*." I dropped my hands to my side and let out a breath. "I can't explain it, but when it comes to anything supernatural, I've always been able to sense it. And not just werewolves, all sorts of creatures."

"Vampires?"

"Huh?"

"Vampires," he said again. "Are those real?"

I opened my mouth, but closed it suddenly. I was taken aback to hear that *that* was the first thing on his mind. But I realized it could've been worse, so I shrugged it off.

"Yeah," I said.

"What about the Swamp Thing?"

"The what?"

"Never mind," he said, his lip curling. "Man, this is wild. You're like a real life ghostbuster."

He began to pace, laughing to himself every few seconds. It wasn't exactly the reaction I was expecting. Then again, I had no *clue* what sort of reaction I was expecting. I'd been hoping that since he was a werewolf, it wouldn't have come as a *complete* shock that I had somewhat of a sixth sense, but I wasn't expecting *laughing*. Even though he was clearly excited, I still wasn't sure how to feel. It was weird; I went my whole life avoiding this topic, and if I ever brought it up to my father at all, he'd fly into a rage. Mick must've noticed my unease because eventually his smile faded.

"Just so you know, I promise not to blab your secret," he said. "And I know you got a hard time keeping your big mouth shut, man, but I'm trusting you not to say anything about me either."

When I realized he was joking, I smiled.

"I won't tell anyone," I said.

"Righteous." He nodded to the headphones around my neck. "So anyway, what's your jam?"

"My what?"

"Your *jam*. What're you listening to?"

"Oh…" I placed a hand on my Walkman, a bit taken aback by the change in topic. "Bruce Springsteen."

"Like, Born in the USA and shit?"

"Uh, yeah."

"Wow," he said, the disappointment in his voice very clear.

"What?"

"It's just…. I never would've pegged you as the type of guy who dug that sort of thing, but hey, who am I to judge? We all got our guilty pleasures, you know what I'm saying?"

"Sure," I said, though I had absolutely no clue what he was talking about.

"What else you into?"

"Umm…" I shrugged. "The Beatles, I guess."

"The *Beatles*?"

"Yeah, is that bad?"

"I wouldn't exactly say bad, man, but that sort of music was written like, a hundred years before we were born. And I'm pretty sure there's a rule or something that says you can't like the same music as your parents." He paused and glanced over his shoulder. "You know what? Come with me."

"Huh?"

"Just trust me," he said, darting off before I could say another word.

For a while, I stared after him until curiosity got the best of me and I followed. When I found him, his nose was buried in a wooden crate that was jam-packed with cassette tapes. He flipped through like a mad man before finally pulling one out and tossing it to me. I bobbled it a moment before holding it steady.

"You ever heard of this band?" he asked.

"*Television*?"

"Yeah, *Marquee Moon*. Totally bangin' album, man. If you're into that lame ol' rock shit, then you're sure to dig this. It's the gateway to punk rock, man. Punk 101. And as long as you promise to give me a full report in chemistry tomorrow, consider it on the house."

My brow lowered. "Can you do that?"

"Do what?"

"I don't know, just give stuff away like that."

He laughed. "Of course I can. I work here. Just don't go narcing on me, and we're all good."

I was unable to contain my smile as I ran my fingers over every last inch of that cassette tape. *Marquee Moon. Television.* The cover was simple—four pale and emaciated guys standing in front of a blue background. But as I began to think about it more, I started to realize there had to be a catch.

"Why're you being so nice to me?" I asked.

He grabbed my shoulder and smirked. "Listen, man. I like you. You're a freak, and I mean that in a good way. Normal people suck. Just relax and quit overthinking everything, got it?"

"Got it."

He slapped my back. "Good. Anyway, it's been real, but I should get back to work before my boss finds out I've been dicking around. I'll see you tomorrow at school though, right?"

"Right."

"Sick, dude. I'm psyched."

As he walked off, I looked at the cassette once more and grinned. Sure, I'd never heard of them before, but I was pretty stoked to give them a try—especially since Mick liked them. Plus, it was nice to add some variety to my musical collection. As much as I loved Bruce, it was time for something new.

When I left the shop, I immediately tore off the plastic wrapping and jammed the tape into my Walkman. It was a chilly night, especially for September. Since it'd rained earlier, the pavement was slick and the air had a fresh earthy scent. There was no doubt it was the perfect night to go on a long walk and listen to some good tunes. But just as I went to start the tape, someone grabbed my shoulder and yanked me back. My heart leapt from my chest as I stumbled into a dark alley and was pushed against the brick wall. There was a hand over my mouth, and I quickly realized it was Scotty.

"Don't scream," he demanded.

I nodded.

He looked at me a moment before dropping his hand.

"I'm sorry for sneaking up on you," he said. "I just wasn't sure of the best way to approach this situation."

"Situation?" I raised my eyebrow. "What situation?"

"Oh, don't play dumb, Charlie," he said. "Ever since I saw you in town the other day, I've been following you. I know everything, so let's cut to the part where we take action. What's the plan?"

"Wait, you've been *following* me?" I asked.

"Yes," he said, "but that's neither here nor there. My point is, I want in."

"In?"

"Yes."

"In *where*?"

He let out a frustrated breath. "As I've previously stated, I've been following you. I'm up to date on all the latest intel. I'm very perceptive, you see. I might not have the gift, but I could still be a viable asset to you." He stopped in front of me, an eerie smile stretched across his face. "I just… I can't believe I've finally found you. After all these years. You and me, Charlie. A *team*."

I blinked a few times. The guy was clearly unhinged. And after the long day I just had, I was not interested in a "team", or whatever it was he was on about. I pushed off the wall and shook my head.

"Thanks but no thanks," I said.

"What?"

"I should get home, but good luck with your thing or whatever."

I marched off and hoped that'd be the end of it, but I had to hand it to him—he was persistent as hell. He followed alongside me, nagging in my ear the entire way.

"Did you hear what I said?" he asked.

"Yep."

"I told you, I could be a great asset to you."

"Not interested."

"Just give me a chance!"

"No."

I placed my headphones over my ears and hoped he'd take the hint, but of course he didn't. In fact, he raised his voice even louder and started grabbing at my arm. I shook him off and pressed on.

It wasn't until we approached a brick overpass that I slowed my pace for the first time. The opening of the dark tunnel was spray-painted to look like a clown's mouth. The graffiti clown had off white skin and thick red lips, the corners runny and smudged. Its eyes were painted a bright yellow with no pupils and looked like two golden orbs. It caused my hair to stand on end. As soon as we strolled right down it's gullet, the shadows engulfed us, and a gentle breeze cut through the air. It felt like a pair of icy fingers tracing along my skin. I pulled my headphones off and looked at Scotty.

"Did you feel that?" I asked

"Feel what?"

"I'm not sure, I think it was—"

Another gust of wind, this time followed by a whisper. I felt a warm breath on the back of my neck, but when I spun around, no one was there.

"Are you okay?" Scotty asked.

"You don't hear that?"

"Hear *what*?"

"That voice!"

"Voice? What voice?"

I held my breath and turned every which way as the whispers grew louder. Panic swept through me. Suddenly, those gentle, icy fingers felt like thick hands wrapped around my neck. I made a break for it. As soon as I reached the light at the end of the tunnel, the whispers ceased abruptly. In their place came a blood-curdling scream. It was so shrill and primal, it turned my blood to ice. I stopped just as something heavy fell from above and landed in front of me with a sickening crunch. An explosion of red liquid shot out like a firework, staining the concrete as well as my shoes and the hem of my jeans.

It didn't take long for me to realize it was blood.

The ride to the police station was a total blur. The only thing I really remembered was the rough polyester of the seats against my skin; it made me itch. I tried to stay calm, but that proved to be harder than I thought as soon as Scotty and I walked into the lobby at the station. They had it organized so all the desks were crammed in one big room which meant officers were rushing around and shouting over one another. There were papers and files scattered everywhere and phones were ringing off the hook; it was total anarchy.

The cop assigned to our case was a large man with a potbelly and a bushy mustache. He wore a silver name tag that read *M. Gibson.* As soon as we sat at his desk, he wasted no time in pulling out a pouch of Beech-nut chewing tobacco and tearing it open.

"Hope you don't mind," he said. "The wife's been on my case to quit smoking."

"Actually," Scotty cut in, "chewing tobacco is just as bad as cigarettes. In fact, there have been countless studies that show it not only leads to mouth cancer, but heart disease and high blood pressure. And since you're already over the recommended weight for someone with your stature, you're basically signing your own death certificate."

Officer Gibson blinked a few times, a look of clear confusion on his face. Scotty on the other hand appeared as cool as a cucumber and looked right back with a pompous grin. Finally, the cop scowled and snatched a nearby can of Tab soda, loudly spit his dip in it, all while never breaking eye contact.

"Why don't we focus on why we're here," he grumbled.

"Fine by me," Scotty said.

The cop reached into his desk drawer and pulled out a notebook and pen. "Now, I understand you're both probably a bit shook up after what you witnessed earlier tonight, so please take your time answering these questions. It's important we work with accurate information."

"I'm not shook up," Scotty said matter-of-factly.

"Excuse me?" the cop asked.

"I said that I am not shook up." He leaned back in his chair and crossed his arms. "Ask away."

The cop glanced at me with his eyebrows raised as if to question Scotty's sanity. To be fair, I really wasn't all that sure myself on whether or not Scotty was right in the head, so I simply shrugged. He eventually shook his head and let out an exasperated breath as he flipped open his pad of paper.

His questions were simple enough, but the more we got into it, the harder I struggled to focus. All I could think about was the sound the body had made as it hit the pavement. The metallic stench that had invaded my nostrils. And when I closed my eyes, all I could see was the bone that'd jutted out from his broken leg. I was super grateful that Scotty took the lead while I simply nodded along. It felt like forever until the officer's radio went off and he excused himself. I sighed in relief as he walked across the room and joined his colleagues. Meanwhile, Scotty scowled after him.

"Bunch of morons," he muttered.

"He's just trying to help," I said.

"Help? Charlie, he's a cop."

"So?"

"*So*? Cops are about as useful as Hitler in a Russian Winter. You heard the guy; he thinks we're dealing with a suicide." He let out a sharp laugh. "Yeah, right."

"Well, it *was* a suicide, wasn't it? I mean, a guy jumped from a bridge. Seems pretty cut and dry."

"Are you for real right now?"

I shrugged.

"God, and I thought you were supposed to be the Venator."

"The what?"

"The Venator!" He threw his hands in the air. "For Christ's sake, Charlie. Why do you keep playing dumb? Is this a test or something?"

I stared blankly. "I honestly have no clue what you're talking about."

"Don't lie to me."

"I'm *not.*"

He crossed his arms and sized me up. The longer he stared, the more aggravated I got. I mean, the guy made absolutely no sense. Always going on and on about the craziest of things as if I was supposed to know what the hell he meant. He must've been looking at me for a solid minute before his expression finally softened.

"You seriously don't know what I'm talking about?" he asked.

"I swear."

"But you can see ghosts, right?"

My mouth fell open, and I quickly snapped it shut. "How'd you—"

He rolled his eyes. "Oh, please. You're not exactly subtle about it. And I'd bet my Colt Python Revolver you can see all sorts of other weird crap, too." He leaned back in his seat and crossed his arms. "Jesus, didn't your dad teach you any of this?"

At the mention of my father, my face grew hot. "Guess not."

"So you know nothing?"

"For the hundredth time," I said. "I have absolutely no clue what the hell you're talking about."

He shook his head. "Sorry, this is just unexpected."

"Well, could you maybe fill me in?"

"Christ…" He ran his fingers through his hair and sighed. "I guess I can give it a try. When I was a kid, my aunt and uncle told me the story about the angel Lucifer who was banished from heaven. As revenge, he plagued the world with evil creatures. Venators were God's response to exterminate that evil. Of course this is the old kiddie folk tale version. It's much more complicated than that, but you get the gist. There's thousands of you, Charlie. And your basic human function is to rid the world of evil. You know, vampires, demons, banshees, maybe even a snallygaster on occasion. It's in your blood. By this point in your life, you're supposed to be a natural born killer, but your dad kind of screwed the pooch on that one. He should've been training you for *years*. Not only how to fight, but how to utilize your powers. Venators not only have the gift of sight, they're also equipped with amazing instincts and heightened senses, but if you don't know what to do with them, then what's the point?"

I rubbed my hands over my face as a wave of nausea passed through me; it was a whole lot to take in. How could my father not tell me any of this? Not one thing. He left me completely in the dark and raised me to feel like a total outcast. In that moment, I hated him more than I ever did before.

"I can't believe this is the first time you're hearing this," Scotty said. "You're so behind. I mean, most Venators start training as young as *four-years-old*."

"Is that when you started?"

"Not exactly," he said, straightening. "But my case is a bit different."

"Why's that?"

He pursed his lips. "Well… because I'm not actually a Venator."

I frowned. "You're not?"

"No."

"Then how the hell do you know all this?"

"It's a long story, but when I was a kid, my mother was killed by a nasty demon and blah, blah, blah. After that, I was taken in by the two Venators who failed to save her. We were close; like family. I even referred to them as my aunt and uncle. I might not have the gift, but I'm about as close as you can get. They taught me everything I know."

"Where are they now?"

"Dead," he said with a straight face.

"*Dead?*"

"Yeah, but it's okay. They were demon hunters which is just about the hardest hunting specialty there is. Quite honestly, it was a wonder they lived as long as they did. Anyway, they left me their trailer with all the equipment and weaponry I'd ever need. I've been hunting here and there, but it's hard because I'm not a Venator and don't know what I'm looking for. It's like stumbling around in the dark. But then I found you, and I was over the moon…" He scrunched his nose. "But Jesus, Charlie. You hardly even have a grasp on the basics. I was definitely not expecting that."

"Thanks," I muttered.

"I'm just speaking the truth," he said. "We could still team up. After all, having a Venator on my side is better than *nothing*."

"Team up?"

"Yes, as in working together to figure out what's been going on around town. It all started with that fire at the theatre followed by these strange weather patterns. And then I saw you staring at that ghost when

I ran into you downtown. I'm guessing it was one of the victims from the fire?"

"Yeah, how'd you know?"

"I told you, I am very perceptive," he said. "Now, I am going to assume you don't know this, but when you see a ghost, that means there was foul play involved with their death. If a person's life has been stolen from them, then they can only move on once their death has been vindicated."

"You mean like murder?"

"Exactly. I have reason to believe that someone started that fire on purpose. And I have no idea how or why, but I believe this fire has something to do with the so-called suicides that've been happening around town. I did some investigating at the scene of the crime and found several traces of wicker."

"Wicker?"

"Yes, there was no mistaking it. You see, wicker might seem harmless enough, but when it's in the wrong hands it's dangerous. It's a highly magical property used mostly with black magic. It was quite popular back in the day with gypsies who used it for voodoo, but it has several other uses as well. Whoever started that fire is up to something, and I have reason to believe they're only getting started."

I held my breath as his last words resonated with me—whoever did this was only getting started. The thought caused my throat to go dry. It wasn't until Officer Gibson returned to his desk and sat down that I was able to refocus.

"Sorry about that," he said. "Anyway, I think we got everything we need for now." He nodded to Scotty. "Since you're eighteen, you're free to go, but your friend's gonna need a parent or guardian to pick him up."

"I'll be eighteen in a few days," I said.

"That's still a minor," he replied.

Scotty shot to his feet and adjusted his trench coat before leaning to my ear. "We'll talk more about this tomorrow. Meet me at the Midtowne trailer park after school. There's something I want to show you." He patted my shoulder and shot the cop one last dirty look before strutting off.

The officer stared after him and frowned. "You really friends with that kid?"

"Guess so," I mumbled.

"My condolences." He snatched the dial phone from the corner of his desk. "Anyway, you got someone we can call?"

"My aunt."

"Where can I reach her?"

"She's at work."

"Yeah, well, where's she work? I'll look her up in the yellow pages."

"The Park," I said. "It's a bar in D.C."

"The *Park*?" He perked up, a slow smile stretched across his face. "You mean the one up in DuPont Circle?"

"Yeah, do you know it?" I asked.

"I know *of* it," he said. "Never been. Not exactly my scene."

He snorted as he flipped through the phone book. I continued to watch with a blank stare as he dialed the number and finally got ahold of her. Turns out, it would take about an hour for her to come get me, so the cop told me to sit tight. I stared after him as he walked off, still laughing to himself. I had absolutely no idea what was so damn funny, but I shrugged it off and made myself comfortable on a bench near the back of the station.

It wasn't until that moment that I realized just how truly wiped I was. The adrenaline must've finally worn off. It felt like I'd just run a marathon or something. I somehow got comfortable despite the pillows feeling like they were made of rocks, and even with all the crazy stuff that was going on, I miraculously found a way to doze off.

I must've been out for longer than I thought, because the next thing I knew there was a high pitched whistle at the front of the station that tore me from my slumber. This was followed by cheers and even more whistles. I sat straight to see what all the commotion was about and it was then that I saw a woman cutting through the crowd. But this wasn't just any woman. No. I'd never seen anything like her before. She had on sparkling red platform heels that had to have added at least eight inches to her already impressive height. She wore ripped fishnet stockings and had on a very short red dress that matched her shoes. Her hair was red and curly and piled on top of her head like a bee hive. Not to mention her makeup was way over the top with thin eyebrows that looked drawn on and arched impossibly high, bright blue eyeshadow, and full lips that were just as sparkly and red as her dress and shoes.

As she cut in front of a group of male officers, one of them whistled particularly loud and said something that made me blush. It hardly even phased her. In fact, she stopped and whipped around so fast, her red hair was like a flash of lightning.

"Ex*cuse* me?" she asked.

"I'm just saying..." He nudged the cop next to him with a smirk. "Those are some nice legs."

"Oh, you wish, honey." Her hand shot to her hip. "Don't think I don't see that cheap arconic wedding ring around your finger. Does your wife know you're a regular in the rainbow room?"

"Oh, umm..." His smile vanished. "N-n-no—"

"Didn't think so," she said. "Next time I hear those filthy words come out of your mouth, you can bet she's going to get a call from a Miss Ophelia Diamonds, you understand, young man?"

He looked to the floor and mumbled something under his breath.

"Sorry, I didn't quite catch that," she snapped.

"Yes, ma'am."

"Good," she said with a wink.

The other officers howled with laughter as she turned on her heel. As she started walking right towards me, I began to realize I'd heard that voice before. In fact, I'd heard it plenty of times, but it wasn't until she stopped right in front of me that I was actually able to piece it all together—it was Aunt Joy. I was hardly able to recognize her face buried underneath all that makeup. Before I could fully process the situation, she wrapped an arm around me and pulled me to my feet.

"You poor thing," she said. "Let's get you home, and I'll cook us some dinner. How does that sound?"

My mouth fell open, but no words came out.

I forced myself to stop staring long enough to follow her to the car. The entire time, she went on about how she'd been worried sick, but it was in one ear and out the other. All I could focus on was how those sparkling heels turned her into an absolute giant. She could hardly even *fit* in the car because her hair was so damn tall. And don't even get me started on her perfume. It was this musky rose scent that made it hard to breathe.

We drove in silence, though I had about a million questions burning through me. Every now and then I stole a glance at her, still in shock that it was actually *her*. There were a few times I could've sworn I saw her reach for the radio volume only to pull her hand away at the last second. It wasn't until we were about halfway home that she took a deep breath and finally found the courage to speak.

"I'm sorry for not telling you sooner," she said.

"Tell me what?"

"About all this," she said, gesturing to her clothes. "I've been avoiding it for far too long, Charlie. I was afraid you'd be embarrassed by me or ashamed, but that's not an excuse. I should've been honest from the start." She paused and bit her lip. "The truth is, I'm a drag queen."

"A what?"

"A drag queen, honey."

"What's that?"

Her head snapped to face me. "You've... you've *never* heard of a drag queen before?"

I shrugged.

She let out a quick laugh and looked back to the road. "Oh wow."

I frowned. "Is that what you do for work or something?"

"Yes, it is," she said. "But there's a bit more to it, I'm afraid. I'm not exactly sure how to put this, so I guess I'm just going to go right ahead and pull the Band-Aid." She took a deep breath. "Honey, a drag queen is a man who dresses in women's clothes as a... form of entertainment."

My brow lowered. "But that doesn't make sense."

"Oh, believe me, sweetie, it does."

"But you're not a...."

"Just take a moment and let it sink in."

"But that would mean..."

"Exactly."

"Oh," I said, my eyes going wide. I quickly looked away from her and stared at the dashboard.

Wow.

So, as it turned out, *she* was really a *he*. The more I thought about it, it explained a whole lot. I mean, she did have some broad shoulders and a husky voice. Then there was the fact that she was always wearing a full face of makeup, even right before bed or as soon as we got up in the morning. The thing was, guy or girl, it didn't change the way I felt about her. I could never hate her. And I didn't want her to think that I did, even for a second. I glanced at her from the corner of my eye and cleared my throat.

"That's cool," I said.

"Oh?"

"Yeah, it really doesn't bother me," I said.

"You mean that?"

"Of course."

She held back a smile, her eyes brimming with tears. "Oh, you're such a sweet boy. I'm just so glad this is out in the open. We're family, Charlie. And family doesn't keep secrets. Promise me from here on out, you and I are going to be honest with each other. How does that sound?"

Honesty. God, that was a tall order. We sat in silence for a few seconds until finally I flashed her the most genuine smile I could muster and nodded.

"Good." She brushed the hair from my face. "I love you, honey."

Those words again. *I love you.* They made my stomach twist.

The rest of the car ride was totally uneventful, thank god. No more wild confessions or dead bodies falling from bridges. I was stoked to finally get home and listen to that cassette tape Mick had got for me. After everything that'd happened, I just needed to clear my head.

Television was *awesome*. They were definitely no Bruce Springsteen, but that wasn't a bad thing. There was this raw energy to them. A take no prisoners' attitude that drew me in. I must've listened to the tape three or four times, mentally taking notes so I'd have something to talk about with Mick the next day. I honestly would've listened to them longer, but I was starting to get too tired to function. I glanced at the clock at my bedside table and realized it was well past midnight.

With a yawn, I slipped off my headphones and tucked my Walkman in my backpack. As I was zipping it up, something out my window caught my eye. It was a light. Edgar's living room. His window was tucked behind some bushes, but given the placement of my room, I could see him clearly. He was hunched over a desk. It appeared as though he was working by a dim lamp light with several melted candles surrounding him.

I inched closer to my window and squinted my eyes.

He was fiddling with a pair of pliers, bending and weaving what looked like pieces of straw into the shape of a tiny doll. The thing was pretty damn creepy. It didn't have a face, and I don't know exactly what it was, but there was just something off about it. After a moment, Edgar held it to the light and smiled before tossing it into a pile of twenty or so other creepy dolls. When he stood, I noticed the torn up basket on the floor behind him. It was hacked and pulled apart.

It was then that it hit me.

I gasped and flicked off the lights. In one quick motion, I ducked below my windowsill and pressed my back against the wall. My chest grew tight, and my mind raced. I was tired. I was paranoid. My mind *had* to be playing tricks on me. But deep down, I knew that wasn't the case. Those creepy dolls weren't made of straw at all.

They were made of wicker.

54

Even though I was exhausted, I couldn't fall asleep that night. Not only did I have to deal with the image of that body as it smacked against the cold hard pavement, I also couldn't seem to forget about those damn wicker dolls.

I walked around like a total zombie all day long. The only thing on my mind was meeting Scotty after school so we could hatch a plan. In fact, I was so wrapped up in all this crap, I totally forgot about my promise to Mick. As our class broke into lab groups, he reminded me with a swift slap to my back.

"So, *Marquee Moon*," he said.

"Huh?" I asked.

"The cassette tape, man. What'd you think?"

"Oh…"

I massaged my hands over my face. *Marquee Moon*. Right. God, it felt like ages ago that I'd listened to that tape, but a promise was a promise. I took a deep breath and focused.

"I liked it," I said finally.

"Yeah?"

"Definitely," I said, my nerves easing as I remembered the music. "They had a really cool sound. Very artsy. I loved the guitar bits. It was different from what I normally listen to, but I liked it."

He clapped his hands together. "I knew it, man. You might seem all shy on the outside, but deep down, you got some edge. You're a real punk rocker."

"I don't know about that," I mumbled, my face red.

"Well, I do," he said. "And you know what? I think you're ready."

"Ready?"

"Yeah, man!"

"For what?"

"Only the single raddest punk band in the whole damn world." He shoved his hand into his backpack and pulled out a cassette tape. "*Misfits*."

Before I could say another word, he tossed it to me. It was all black with red lettering and a picture of a skeleton that immediately reminded me of one of Mick's horror t-shirts. I flipped it over and read a few of the track listings—*Astro Zombies, Horror Business, Teenagers from Mars, Spinal Remains, Halloween*. In the margins were illegible pen scribbles and hand drawn pictures of skulls and a huge middle finger.

"You play?" Mick asked.

"Huh?"

"Guitar, man. I noticed at *Blue Dog* last night you were checking out a primo Martin acoustic. I figured with taste like that, you knew a thing or two."

"I guess I play a little."

"You ever play with a band?"

I shook my head.

He smirked. "Well, that's gotta change, man. My friends and I got this band and we've been looking for a second guitar for ages. You think you'd be into giving it a go? I'd really owe you one."

My heart skipped a beat. His band. He wanted me to play with his *band*. The idea had me totally amped and wanting to barf at the same time.

"I don't know," I said.

"Why not?"

"It's just... I'm not very good."

He let out a sharp laugh. "Well, then you'd fit right in. We suck. But no one gives a shit when you're rockin' out with your friends. After school, man, I'll introduce you to Steve and Andy. We're meeting up at *The Guillotine* for some burgers then heading to *Blue Dog* after to jam."

"Today?"

"Yeah, today. What, you got something better to do?"

For a brief moment, I thought about Scotty, but before I could say a word, he slapped my back.

"Righteous," he said. "It's settled then. We'll head on over once school's out."

My mouth was still hanging open when he snatched the cassette from my hands and began going over every single track and why it was significant to the punk world. He was so damn excited; I just didn't have the heart to tell him no.

When the bell finally rang, he practically dragged me down the hallway. He spoke so fast, I began to worry I'd never muster the courage to mention that I'd already had plans with Scotty. But a funny thing happened as we walked outside; I started to care less and less. And then suddenly, I didn't care at all. So what if I didn't meet with Scotty? Whatever was going on around town—that was if there even was something—was not my responsibility. And if I was being totally honest, I was pretty amped to hang out with Mick. This was what normal looked like. Normal kids hung out with their friends after school. Normal kids weren't worrying about black magic or spirits or wicker curses. Besides, Scotty had a handle on it. He said it himself, I hardly had a grasp on the basics. It wasn't like I was going to be of much help anyway. The more I thought about it, the more I convinced myself I was doing the right thing.

As Mick and I made our way downtown, he continued talking my ear off about all sorts of things—his top ten favorite horror films which included *The Creature from the Black Lagoon* and *Forbidden World*; his vast collection of *Swamp Thing* comic books; and of course, his prized possession which was a left-handed red Fender Mustang. We walked side by side, the air cool and damp from an earlier storm.

"So, what's your deal?" Mick asked out of the blue.

"What do you mean?"

"I don't know," he said with a shrug. "Like, where are you from? You ever been to NoVa before? You got a *dog* or some shit? Just, whatever, man. You never talk about yourself. I wanna know more."

I frowned and looked at my feet. There wasn't a whole lot to say. I mean, I was pretty boring aside from the whole supernatural thing, and he already knew about that. I kicked a rock down the street and blurted out the first thing that came to mind.

"I live with my aunt," I said.

"No parents?"

I shook my head.

"Why not?"

I was kind of taken aback with his lack of tact. Or maybe I was just being too sensitive. Who knows? I shoved my hands in my pockets and forced the words out quickly.

"My mom died when I was born," I said.

"And your dad?"

"I used to live with him, but now I live with my aunt."

"What happened?"

I chewed my lip. "He did something bad, so I got taken away."

He stared at me a moment before letting out a sharp laugh. "Jesus, man. Throw me a bone."

"What do you mean?"

"You're so damn cryptic. I just can't get a read on you."

"Sorry," I muttered.

"*Sorry*? Come on, man! Don't apologize. Never apologize." He nodded to my cheek bone. "Those stitches. Is that the bad thing you were talking about?"

I froze up like a total spaz-oid. I could feel him gawking at me, but I kept my eyes locked on my shoes and my lips pressed together tightly.

"I can tell you don't like talking about this," he said finally.

"I don't."

"Why not? It ain't good to bottle all this shit up. Maybe it's why you're so tense all the time." He ran his fingers through his hair and sighed. "Listen man, you got nothing to be embarrassed about. No one's got a perfect home life. If they did, people would live with their parents forever. I mean, I love my mom to death, but she's a total wreck. She can't take care of herself, let alone me. And then my dad walked out on my mom and me a few years back, but even before that he was a total prick. Screw them both, man. And screw your parents, too. Good friends are all you really need. Friends you can trust. Like, take me for example. Whenever a full moon rolls around, you think I ask my *mom* to tranq me? Hell no! My friends are the ones who got my back."

"Wait, they *tranq* you?"

He smirked. "Yeah, man. With a tranquilizer gun. It's some real *Terminator* shit. We got this wicked dart gun and make a night of it. I'll have to show you next time a full moon rolls around."

"So, your friends know about the whole...."

"Werewolf thing?"

"Yeah."

"Of course they do. That's the thing about good friends, man. When the whole world goes to shit, they're the ones you can trust. Speaking of which…" He stopped in front of a big red door and held up his hands. "Get ready for some damn good burgers with the best group of assholes you'll ever meet."

"We're here?"

"Yeah, man. Welcome to *The Guillotine*."

I looked up at the giant neon sign hanging over the front door. The name of the place made a lot more sense once I walked in and saw the huge wooden guillotine on display in the center of the room. It was surrounded by booths and tables packed to the brim with kids I'd seen around school. Their loud chatter was mixed with the sound of burgers sizzling on open grills and a jukebox humming rock music. Every last square inch of the walls were plastered with colorful scribbles which upon closer inspection I realized were names and quick notes written in marker and crayon. Things like *Fuck Midtowne High School* in big bold letters. Below that was a set of initials with a heart around it. One of the initials had a thick black line through it and the words *cheating scum* written above.

Mick nudged my arm. "You see that big ass guillotine?"

"Yeah," I said.

"My friends and I signed our names right below it," he said. "Best spot in the house. We were actually the first ones to write on the walls. It just sort of caught on and now everyone does it."

He perked up and waved at two people near the back corner before turning to me and lowering his voice.

"All right," he said, "the chick's name is Andy, and the dude's Steve. Just a heads up, Steve's probably gonna bust your balls, but don't let it get to you. He means well. He's just.... Steve."

Before I could process what he'd just said, he grabbed my arm and yanked me along.

We stopped in front of a corner booth. There sat who I presumed to be Andy and Steve. The first thing I noticed was Andy's electric blue pixie hair. Her skin was olive in tone and made me think she might've been Puerto Rican or something along those lines. She was small and thin and wore a green army jacket over a white Patti Smith t-shirt. Steve on the other hand was tall and lanky, his black hair shaved into a Mohawk. He had on a torn up leather jacket plastered with patches and spikes along the shoulder. When the two of them spotted me, they stopped talking and immediately straightened.

Mick placed a hand on my shoulder and grinned. "Guys, meet Charlie. He's my lab partner."

"*Lab* partner?" Steve asked.

"Yeah," Mick said. "And he's cool as hell, so he's gonna hang with us for a bit."

Mick sat and nodded for me to join him. I grit my teeth and slid into the booth next to him. There was a painfully awkward silence as I glanced from Andy to Steve and suddenly had no idea what to do with my hands. I placed them on the table, but that didn't feel right, so I put them in my lap. I must've looked like a total idiot fumbling back and forth until Steve finally broke the silence.

"Gnarly stitches," he said, nodding to my cheekbone. "So, what's the story?"

"The what?" I asked.

"The *story*, man! Behind every bruise, cut, or broken bone, there's always a killer story. Like, one time I went bowling with my little bro. The ball was tiny as hell, so when he went to roll it, that shit got caught on his fingers and he ended up breaking his nose on the follow through. But dude, that shit was hilarious! He had a nose cast for weeks."

"He needed surgery after that," Andy said.

"So?" he asked.

"So, it was pretty serious," she answered.

"Yeah, seriously *hilarious*." He let out an obnoxious laugh and turned back to me. "So, Charlie, my man, what's the story? You get in a fight, or was this more of a bowling ball to the noggin type sitch?"

I blushed. The story. God, there was absolutely no way in hell I was going to dive into that cesspit of despair. I wasn't really sure what to do and everyone was staring at me. I felt the pressure mounting and forced my mouth open, but the only thing that came out was a bunch of stammering.

"He doesn't like talking about it," Mick cut in.

"He doesn't like talking at all," Steve mumbled.

Mick scowled. "Don't worry about that, man. The kid can shred on guitar! That's all that really matters, right?"

"He shreds?" Andy asked.

"Totally," Mick said, grabbing my shoulder. "And he's gonna be jamming with us over at *Blue Dog* later. He's kind of new to the punk scene, but it's cool. I've been teaching him a thing or two."

Steve smirked. "Oh, *you've* been teaching him? Let me guess, you leant him that old-ass *Misfits* tape?"

"Yeah, so?" Mick asked.

"So, it's a little worn out," he answered. "I mean, we made that mix back in the *sixth* grade."

"*And?*" Mick snapped.

"I'm just saying," Steve said, "*Misfits* are a solid band and all, but—"

"Don't you dare!" Mick said, covering his ears.

Steve raised his voice. "This is an intervention, dude! You need to hear this! *Misfits* are totally sick, but there's plenty of other bands out there!"

At this point, Mick began singing at the top of his lungs. Steve shouted even louder and attempted to yank Mick's hands from his ears.

I couldn't help but smile.

"Ignore them," Andy said, nudging my foot under the table. "So, what kinda music do you like, Charlie?"

"Me?"

She smirked. "Yeah, the quiet one with the curly hair."

My smile faded as I shifted in my seat. "Well, umm, Mick leant me *Marquee Moon* the other day."

"That's Mick. I'm asking about you. What's your style?"

"Oh…." I pressed my lips together and thought for a moment. "I like Bruce Springsteen."

"Favorite album?"

"*Born to Run.*"

She looked me up and down, and it was then that I started to realize just how much I wanted her to like me. And not just her, Mick and Steve, too. God, I was so damn pathetic. She could probably sense my desperation.

"That's a great choice," she said, her lip curling.

"It is?" I asked.

"Yeah," she said. "Totally rad."

"Oh, ummm…" I shifted in my seat. "Thanks."

Totally rad. She thought I was totally *rad*. But then again, she could have just meant that the album was rad. That was probably it. All the same, I couldn't help but smile.

Mick shoved Steve off once and for all, his face red from fighting and laughing. Steve snuck a few jabs to Mick's side before turning to me with a grin.

"So, Charlie," he said, "What I'm trying to say is the Misfits are good and all—"

"Great," Mick interrupted.

Steve rolled his eyes. "Great. Fine. Whatever. I'm just trying to say, Charlie man, you need to branch out. We're living in D.C. for Christ's sake. It's the mecca for some of the best hardcore bands of this decade. You got *Bad Brains, Dag Nasty, Minor Threat, Soulside*—I could go on and on. Fast, hard, aggressive, in-your-fucking-face lyrics. That's what punk's all about, dude."

"Don't forget, it's anti-establishment," Andy added. "Anarchy. Rebellion. Fuck Reagan and his damn Reaganomics. Fuck Margaret Thatcher. Fuck all the yuppie materialistic assholes. It's about rejecting societal standards. And don't even get me started on how hard women get the shaft, especially in the music industry. There are so many great chick rockers that don't get the respect they deserve, it's insane. We need to expose you to some Siouxsie Sioux or some Mia Zapata and Gina Birch, stat."

"For sure," Mick said. "And we'll get to all that soon enough. But right now, we need to order some goddamn burgers before I pass the hell out."

I didn't really realize just how hungry I was until I took my first bite of food. The burger was so damn big, I could only eat half. The others didn't seem to have the same problem I did and finished their meals within minutes, even munching on a plate of cheese fries Mick insisted we get. As we digested our meals, I sipped at my soda and watched while they argued over the greatest movie of all time. Mick was a firm believer in *Evil Dead*, which as he put it, was the best solely based on the fact that it held the record for most fake blood used in a single scene. Steve on the other hand was partial to the *Halloween* movies while Andy was all about *The Rocky Horror Picture Show.* And the lengths at which they went to defend their point of view was hilarious to watch. At one point, I even had to duck beneath the table to avoid being a casualty when Steve threw a handful of fries at Mick. They sort of ignored me for the most part, but I didn't really mind. I just liked being around them.

After we cleared our table, we walked across the street to *Blue Dog.* There was a guy working behind the counter, but other than that, the place was pretty empty. Mick took us to a back corner where a bunch of instruments were buried beneath discount stickers and signs. Andy and Steve hopped on top of a dusty old amp while Mick snatched a sunburst electric guitar from a nearby stand.

"I got a pretty sick deal with my boss," he said. "I'm allowed to screw around on the used instruments in exchange for working a few extra hours a week for free." He plugged the guitar into a small amp before holding it out to me. "Have at it."

My eyes grew wide. "Me?"

"Yeah, you."

"Right now?"

"No, next week," he said with a smile. "Of course right now, man! Come on, I wanna hear you shred."

I looked at the guitar then back to Mick. It'd been months since I'd practiced, but even with all the practice in the world, I was never really that good. And I most definitely didn't *shred*. After a moment, I shook my head.

"I can't," I said.

"Why not?" he asked.

"I suck."

"Don't worry about that," he said. "No one's gonna judge you, man." He gave me a nod and gestured once more for me to take the guitar. "Just play."

I took a deep breath and looked at the instrument. Despite it being used, the wood was sleek, and the strings were tight. Before I could change my mind, I snatched the guitar and swung the strap over my head. Steve and Andy broke into cheers, but I ignored them and gripped the neck. *Just Play*. Right. It sure sounded easy, but it wasn't.

With a deep breath, I began to strum the first thing that came to mind which was *Black Mountain Side* off of *Led Zeppelin's* first album. I started slowly, but the longer I played, the more I lost myself and soon enough, the tension just disappeared. It was *amazing*. God, I missed playing. When I was finally done, I let the guitar hang around my neck and basked in the euphoric feeling. It wasn't until I heard Andy's sharp whistle that I fully came back down to earth.

"Dude," Steve said, his eyes wide. "You're a *beast*!"

"Yeah," Andy added. "Very impressive."

"Told you," Mick said.

I mumbled my thanks and rubbed the back of my neck. I knew they were just being nice, but all the same, there was no hiding how red I was.

"Ain't no doubt you got talent," Steve said, "But punk ain't about hitting all the right notes. It's about playing with emotion. Attitude. You're way too tight, dude. We gotta loosen those edges."

Andy hopped off the amp and walked toward me. "Yeah, he's right. Maybe don't stand so straight."

"Bend your knees," Mick said, rushing to my side. He crouched down and forced my feet apart. "Jesus, you're like Mr. Roboto, man. Ease up."

"Your hair," Andy said, her nose wrinkled.

"And your *shirt*," Mick added.

Before I knew it, they were ruffling their hands through my hair and tugging at my clothes, laughing. Every few seconds they'd dramatically gasp or fuss about something else, and it wasn't long until I was smiling along with them. When they were finally done, they stepped back and looked me over.

"You think that's better?" Andy asked.

"Let's see." Mick crossed his arms. Strike a chord, Charlie man."

Without changing my pose, I struck a simple chord. The sound reverberated from the amp. I looked back at them, but they didn't seem all that impressed.

"Do it again," Mick demanded.

"Yeah," Andy said, rubbing her chin, "and this time, slouch a bit."

I did my best to hunch my shoulders and strummed once more. Before I could even hit all six strings, Mick made me go again. Then again. And then *again*. He was barking at me to strum faster and harder, and it wasn't long before Andy joined in. Faster. Harder. *Faster. Harder.* I felt like I was at boot camp. They were jumping up and down and shouting at the top of their lungs while I strummed as fast as I possibly could. Just when I thought my hand would fall off, they fell onto each other and began cracking up. I watched with a smile until Steve stepped in front of me.

"That's not it," he said, his tone oddly sharp.

It could've been the way he scowled or maybe it was the fire in his eyes, but whatever it was caused me to tense up. He looked me up and down for an uncomfortably long time before finally scoffing.

"Why are you so damn quiet?" he asked.

"Oh…." I took a step back and shuffled my feet. "I'm… erm. I'm not sure."

"It's annoying," he snapped.

"Sorry," I muttered.

"You're *sorry*?"

"Y-yeah, I—"

"Speak the hell up." He snapped his fingers in my face. "I'm sick of all this timid bullshit, dude. Grow some balls."

"Yo, take it easy, man," Mick said, stepping in.

"Yeah," Andy added. "Chill out."

Steve ignored them and locked his eyes on mine. "You let everyone walk all over you. I bet you've never stood up for yourself a day in your pathetic life." His lip curled suddenly. "So, who cut up your face? Was it some kid at your last school? Let me guess, you *let* him beat the piss out of you like the doormat you are. Yeah, I bet you didn't do shit about it. Tell me I'm wrong."

I opened my mouth but closed it suddenly. He was right; I was a total doormat. Even now, I was too afraid to look him in the eye. I kept as still as possible and hoped like hell he couldn't hear my heart thundering.

"That's what I thought," he said, and to my surprise he snuck a quick and painful jab to my shoulder.

"Ouch," I said.

"You're not gonna do shit." He shoved me again, this time harder. "Come on, don't be a pussy. Stand up for yourself."

"Steve, that's enough," Andy demanded.

He ignored her and struck my chest again, causing me to stumble back. My foot hit a stray cord, and I barely caught myself before he shoved me again.

"You're just gonna let me push you around?" He jabbed my shoulder again. "Come on, dude. Stand up to me. Don't be a pussy!" Another sharp jab. "Tell me to fuck off, I dare you! Say it!"

He continued to poke and prod my arm and chest until it was sore. It was hard not thinking about my father. All those times he berated me. Made me feel small. The more I thought about it, the hotter my blood boiled. My father shouting in my face. My father kicking me. Hitting me. Calling me names. And I never stood up to him. Not once.

Steve was right.

It was like I was transported through time and space and was back in my old trailer. In a flash of rage, I shoved him as hard as I could and screamed at the top of my lungs. It was a volcano erupting. Seventeen damn years of pent up anger released in a single moment. I blinked a few times as the adrenaline faded. I saw Steve. He was standing in front of me, wide-eyed. It was then that I realized my fists were clenched so tight, they were shaking. I eased my grip and took a deep breath.

"Sorry," I muttered.

"Don't be," Steve said as he prodded my chest. "You feel that?"

"Feel what?"

"That raw, unadulterated emotion," he said. "That pure *fucking* anger. That right there is punk rock. It's about waking people's consciousness. An assault on the senses. It demands to be heard. I knew you had it in you, you just needed some help tapping into it."

I stared at him. That anger. He was right. I'd always felt it bubbling beneath the surface. God, it felt so good to finally let it the hell out.

"We cool?" he asked, holding out his hand.

I stared at it a moment before slapping it. "Yeah, we're cool."

He swung his arm around me. "Hell yeah. You're one bomb ass dude, Charlie. But just a word of advice. Next time someone gets all up in your grill like that, you deck that mother fucker. Even if it's me. Got it?"

I nodded.

Mick shook his head in disbelief. "You know, in a weird, twisted way, that was sort of beautiful."

Steve shrugged. "I have my moments."

Andy rolled her eyes. "Well, I still think you're a dick."

He grabbed a nearby bass and swung the strap over his head. "I can't really argue with that. But enough with the bullshit. We gonna jam or what?"

I used to think that playing music by myself was beyond awesome, but it was nothing compared to playing in a band. We played well after the store closed, which was fine by me; I never wanted to leave. Steve was wild on the bass, always jumping and dancing. Andy was a badass drummer and played loud, hard, and fast. And then Mick had much more talent than he let on. He not only played guitar, but sang, too. His voice was smooth and deep, almost like a young Jim Morrison.

By the end of the night, I just couldn't stop smiling. In fact, I don't think I've ever smiled so much in my entire life. We walked home that night, disappearing one by one until it was just me and Mick. As he walked up the stone path to his house and I was finally alone, I took a moment to breathe. Just *breathe*. It was a quiet night, but a good sort of quiet. Peaceful. There was a cool breeze, the crickets were chirping, and for the first time in my life, everything felt right.

I was alive.

I grabbed the *Misfits* cassette Mick had leant me from my backpack and slipped it in my Walkman before pressing play and starting the walk home.

Misfits were a step up from *Television*. Not only were they faster and louder, the lyrics were way more aggressive. The first song on the cassette, *Spinal Remains*, set the tone. *And I will not sit on broken glass. Not for you or anyone. I will not cut my fucking ass.* It was so gritty and raw. Never in a million years would I have thought that I'd like that sort of music, but I did. I really did. And I was so damn excited for seventh period chemistry so I could talk about it more with Mick.

First though, I had to get through lunch.

Just like every other day I was on my way to the library where I'd find a table in the back to quietly munch on whatever Aunt Joy had packed for the day and catch up on some homework. But just as I grabbed a few things from my locker, someone shoved into me. There was laughter as my books were knocked from my hands. There stood two guys from my third period gym class. The one who'd knocked my books to the floor was short but stocky with gorilla arms and a red letterman jacket while the other was skinny with a long, greasy mullet.

"Watch where you're going, new kid," the one with the gorilla arms said.

"Yeah, spaz," his friend chimed in.

They continued to laugh as I pressed my lips together. What I really wanted to do was tell them to get bent, but of course I stood there like a total moron while they hurled insults at me.

"You gonna say anything?" the mullet asked.

"Nah, I think he's a mute," the gorilla said, leaning close to my face. "Or maybe he's retarded."

The tension built as he glared at the side of my head. I didn't dare look at him and instead kept my eyes glued to the ground. Just when I thought I'd pass out from the stench of his nasty Dorito breath, Steve strolled in with a cocky grin and casually leaned against the lockers. That afternoon, he was wearing a sleeveless Black Flag t-shirt with suspenders and his mohawk gelled into crazy spikes.

"Hey Charlie," he said before glancing at my tormentors. "I see you've made some new friends."

"Get lost, Steve," the gorilla said. "This is none of your business."

"Oh, but I think it is," Steve said.

He pushed off the lockers and stood straight. It wasn't until that moment that I realized just how tall he actually was. He might've been lanky, but he had a good five or six inches on both of them. They exchanged a nervous glance as Steve looked at my books and pens scattered on the ground.

"Oh, my, my," he said. "And what happened here?"

"Nothing," the gorilla mumbled.

"Gee, it sure doesn't look like nothing." He grabbed my shoulder. "In fact, it kinda looks like you've been baggin' on my new best friend here. Now, I'm sure you and Biff Tannen over there didn't mean it, but just in case, I'm gonna kindly ask you to apologize."

Gorilla-boy scoffed. "You serious?"

Steve scowled. "Dead serious. And while you're at it, you two butt-munchers can pick up his books, too." He cracked his knuckles. "Unless, of course, you'd rather settle this another way?"

At this point, a crowd of onlookers were surrounding us and the hallways filled with whispers. The gorilla looked Steve up and down as if weighing his options, and for a brief moment, I thought he might actually throw a punch. But then he cursed under his breath and much to my disbelief, crouched down to pick up my things.

"Don't forget that pen over there," Steve said with a shit-eating-grin.

The asshole rolled his eyes, but sure enough, picked up the pen and handed it to me. Steve crossed his arms and watched with a satisfied smirk until all my things were off the floor. He then forced both of them to apologize not once, but twice. As they trudged down the hall in defeat, I couldn't help but smile.

Once the crowd realized there wasn't going to be a fight, the whispers faded and everyone went back to their business. Not sure what else to do, I adjusted my grip on my books and made a move to go to the library, but before I could even take a step, Steve stuck out his hand.

"Whoa there, Charlie boy," he said. "Where you going?"

"The library," I said.

"The *library*?"

"Yeah, for lunch."

He stared at me with a stunned expression. "Dude, there is no way in hell I'm gonna let you eat lunch in the library."

"Why not?" I asked.

"Because that's depressing as shit," he said. "No *way*. No. From now on, you eat with us." He grabbed my arm and yanked me down the hallway. "For Christ's sake, dude. I didn't know even know this school *had* a fucking library."

He moved so fast, I didn't really have a chance to say no. Not that I would've. I might've been nervous, but the idea of eating lunch with him was way too exciting to pass up.

The second we walked into the cafeteria, it was like being hit with a tidal wave of noise. People were screaming, running around, throwing food—it was a jungle. Total anarchy. Steve started jabbering about the inner works of it all which was much more intricate and organized than I had thought. Every single table and corner of the lunchroom belonged to a different clique—jocks, nerds, stoners, teacher's pets. I was just starting to wonder where Steve sat when we blew right past all the tables and out the side door to a small courtyard.

"I thought we were gonna eat in the cafeteria," I said.

"Screw the cafeteria," he said. "We're going to the shed."

"The *what*?"

"The shed. Only dweebs eat in the cafeteria, dude. Trust me."

"Oh…. right," I said.

We continued walking along the side of the building until we turned a corner, and that's when I saw it—the shed from hell. The thing looked straight out of a horror movie. It was tucked next to a broken chain link fence that was swarmed by overgrown grass and weeds. Sitting beneath the clouded windows of the shed were a couple of students wearing all black and smoking cigarettes. It was then I spotted Mick lying on a stone ledge and tossing an apple up and down. Andy was on the ground next to him nibbling a sandwich. Steve grabbed my arm and dragged me right over.

"Look who I found," he said as we stopped in front of them. "This little rascal was trying to pick a fight with Kenny Toddleson and that little butt buddy he's always hanging around with."

"The one with the mullet?" Mick asked.

"That's the one," Steve said.

My eyes grew wide. "Oh, I wasn't trying to—"

Steve slapped my back. "Nonsense. Anyway, ol' Charlie boy had it handled. Yeah, by the time I got there, both those goons were on their hands and knees picking up his shit for him. He didn't need me."

"No way," Mick said.

"Yes way, dude." Steve turned so only I could see and winked. "I know he might not look like much, but Charlie here's a silent killer. Ain't no one messes with him."

"That's badass, man," Mick said.

"Yeah," Andy added, taking a bite of her sandwich. "Normally I don't condone senseless violence, but those jerks had it coming. They're always ganging up on people. Good on you for standing up to them, Charlie."

I looked to my shoes and blushed. "Thanks."

Steve tossed his paper lunch bag on the ground and stretched out next to Andy. He was already tearing open a snack sized bag of *Ruffles* potato chips and stuffing his face when he motioned for me to join them. I took a deep breath, placed my books down, and took a seat next to him.

"What's with the books?" Mick asked.

"Oh, dude," Steve said, his mouth full. "Get this. Charlie here's been eating his lunch in the damn library the past few weeks. Can you believe that?"

"Since when did this school get a library?" Mick asked.

Steve snorted. "That's what I said!"

Andy rolled her eyes. "You know, both of you could stand to read a book or two. It's like talking to a wall anytime I try to discuss interventionist American foreign policy or social conservatism. You'd think as hardcore punk rockers you two might actually care about our current political climate."

"Say what now?" Steve asked.

"My point exactly," she said.

Mick clapped his hands together. "Library or not, I think we can all agree that Charlie should be eating lunch with us from here on out. We're a band now, so it only makes sense. Speaking of which, Charlie man, what're you doing Friday night?"

I shrugged. "Nothing, I guess."

"Great," Mick said. "This Friday we're hanging out at my place. You in?"

Andy's eyes widened, and she punched Mick's arm. "I thought we were playing *darts* Friday."

"We are," he said. "So?"

She pursed her lips. "So, what about your *dog*? You know, the huge furry one that looks like a *wolf*?"

"Oh, that," he said, waving his hand. "Don't worry, Charlie knows about the whole werewolf thing."

"He *what*?" she asked.

"Dude," Steve said, his jaw dropped, "You told him?"

"Guys, take it easy," he said. "I mean, it's not like I told him on purpose. The kid just sort of figured it out. He has this thing where he can see vampires and ghosts and shit." His smile vanished. "Oh, shit, sorry, man. Didn't mean to blab." He turned back to the others and shook his head. "No one bug him. He doesn't like talking about it."

"Don't *bug* him?" Andy asked.

"You gotta be kidding," Steve said. "You just dropped a mondo nuke on us, dude. Like, what the hell do you mean he can see vampires?"

"And ghosts," Andy added.

Steve's head snapped to me. "Shit, are *you* a ghost?"

They fired off question after question, and my heart raced. I looked to Mick who gave me an apologetic shrug, but there wasn't much more he could do. It was too late. They knew my secret. It all happened so fast, I'd barely had time to process it.

"So, you gonna give us the dirty deets or what?" Steve asked.

"Yeah," Andy said. "Don't leave us hanging, Charlie. You can trust us. We're your friends now."

Dammit.

She knew my weakness. *Friends.* It was like the magic key that finally got me to open up. With a deep breath, I dug my fingers into my legs and forced myself to speak. I told them everything, though I left out the bits about the suicides and theatre fire for now. There was no need for them to worry about something that probably didn't even have anything to do with me. When all was said and done, I was met with complete silence, though it was clear they were stoked. I was terrified of what they might think, but come to think of it, I wasn't sure why. Their obsession with scary movies and horror punk should've indicated that they'd be totally on board for everything.

"Dude, this is fucking righteous," Steve said. "So, you're a Venator that comes from a long line of blood-sucking, ass-kicking, monster-slaying-badasses, and you're just mentioning this *now*?"

"I guess so," I said.

"That's totally punk rock," Andy added. "I mean, a werewolf and a monster slayer in the same band, how rad is that?"

"It's mad legit," Mick said.

They went on about how cool I was for a solid minute while I stared in shock. After a moment, Steve messed up my hair, and an inevitable smile spread across my face. I turned to Mick who flashed me a grin and gave me a thumbs up. It was then that it really hit me; things were going to be okay.

We spent the rest of lunch discussing Friday night. Apparently it was a full moon, so that meant Mick would be changing into a werewolf. The craziest part was how casual they were about it all. Andy promised she'd walk me through the whole process with the dart gun and whatnot and assured me I wouldn't be in any real danger, though I wasn't sure how that was possible. I'd never seen a werewolf up close, but from what I knew about them, I imagined they were anything but safe.

I was disappointed when the school bell rang; I could've spent all day out in that courtyard. We collected our things and were just opening the side door to go back inside when I felt a hand on my shoulder. I spun around, my heart skipping a beat when I saw Scotty standing before me. His face was sullen and worn, his beige trench coat disheveled and black boots untied. In an instant, all the excitement I had once felt was just sucked away.

"We need to talk," he said.

Before I could answer, Steve stepped between us. "Charlie man, you know this kid?"

Scotty crossed his arms. "He does. So, if you don't mind, we have some business to attend to."

"*Business?*" Steve asked.

"Yes, he replied, "And I'd appreciate some privacy."

Steve raised his eyebrow and glanced at me. "Yo, just say the word, dude, and I'll get rid of him."

"*Pft,*" Scotty said. "If I wanted, I could—"

"It's all right," I said, yanking Scotty's arm. "I know him. I'll catch up with you guys later."

I dragged Scotty to a nearby oak tree as he shot my friends daggers. I waited as the rest of the students filed inside one by one, and when I was sure we were alone, I crossed my arms and sighed.

"What do you want?" I asked.

"That's all you have to say after ditching me yesterday?"

"I didn't ditch you."

"Oh, really?" His hands shot to his hips. "We had plans to meet yesterday, but you blew me off for a cheap hamburger and french fries. Kind of sounds like ditching to me. And what the hell are you doing hanging around with Mick Gallagher anyway? He's bad news. And those friends of his. Jesus, Charlie, they're total degenerates."

"They're not degenerates."

"Sure they are," he said. "I mean, just *look* at them for Chrissakes."

"They're just…" I narrowed my eyes. "Hang on, how'd you know where I was yesterday?"

"Because I followed you," he said matter-of-factly.

"You *what?*"

"Oh, quit acting so surprised. If you haven't already noticed, I do it a lot." He threw his hands in the air and scoffed. "I just don't get it. This was important. Why'd you ditch me like that?"

"Because," I said, rubbing my hands over my face. I was never one to be blunt, but this was something he needed to hear. I figured it'd be best to rip it off like a Band-Aid, so with a deep breath, I forced the words out quickly. "Listen, Scotty, this whole thing with the fire and the suicides—it's none of our business. You and me, we're in *high school*. How're we supposed to help?"

"Speak for yourself," he said. "I might be young, but I've been fully trained."

"Then you do it. Why do you even need me?"

"Because you're a Venator."

"So?"

"So, this is what you were born to do!" He pushed his hair from his face and sighed. "Listen, as much as I hate to admit it, I can train until

I'm blue in the face, but it doesn't matter. Without the gift, I'm blind.
You're my eyes, Charlie. And I can't believe you'd rather screw around
with Billy Idol than fulfill your destiny."

"This isn't our problem," I said, my fists clenched. "Besides, who
said any of this has to do with my "gift" or whatever anyway? I mean,
for all we know, it doesn't. Let the cops figure it out."

"Screw the cops, they—"

"No," I said, my tone sharp. "And I'm done talking about this, all
right? I have to get to class."

He grabbed my arm before I could leave. "What about the sun?"

"What about it?" I asked.

"I doubt you've noticed, but there hasn't been a single day of light
since the theatre fire. Not one. It's either been cloudy or rainy. We've
been living in total darkness. It's all over the news, not to mention I've
been tracking weather patterns and compared to past years, this is
completely abnormal."

"Who cares?"

"Who *cares*? Are you dense? This is hitting you square in the face,
but you refuse to see it. Don't you think it's at least a little bit strange
this is all happening after a random fire started by wicker?"

I pressed my lips together, not sure what to say. Sure, a small part
of me sensed that maybe something was up, but there was an even
bigger part that wanted nothing to do with any of it. This was my
chance to be normal. To have friends. And I'd more than paid my dues
by living with my father for the past seventeen goddamn years. Let me
tell you, after that, I was done with the supernatural world for good. I
thought back to what Steve had said about standing up for myself and
realized this moment was as good as any.

"It's not strange at all," I said.

"Oh, come on, you have to—"

"I don't *have* to do anything," I snapped. "Why don't you just mind your damn business?"

I turned on my heel and marched off.

As it turned out, Mick didn't live too far from me, so on Friday, I decided to walk straight to his place after school. To accompany me, I picked out the cassette tape Steve had lent me—*First Two Seven Inches* by a band called *Minor Threat*. He told me it was one of his favorite D.C. hardcore bands, and I soon figured out why. The first song was a super short burst of pure aggression. *What happened to you? You're not the same. Something in your head made a violent change.* It was different than anything I'd ever heard before, but it reminded me of Steve, so I liked it. All the songs had to have been less than two minutes long, so by the time I got to Mick's, I'd pretty much listened to the entire tape.

When I approached his front door, I pulled off my headphones, and a rush of nerves swelled in my stomach. I'd never been to a sleepover before, let alone one with a frickin' werewolf. I wasn't sure what to expect, but I did my best to ignore those fears and knocked. All too fast, the door swung open, and a breath caught in my lungs. Standing before me was an older woman. She was frail and hunched over wearing nothing but a thick fleece nightgown. Her hair was a ratty gray nest atop her head, and I don't know how to describe it, but the look in her eyes told me she wasn't all there.

"Can I help you?" she asked.

"I'm Charlie," I said, and when she continued to stare, I added, "Mick's friend."

"Oh, Mickey?" Her lips curled into a faint smile. "He's such a sweetheart. I sure do miss that boy."

"Huh?"

"My darling, Mickey. You'll tell him I said hello, won't you?"

I frowned and glanced over my shoulder thinking maybe I had the wrong house, but the mailbox read 231 East 47th Street. I had the right address, or at least I thought I did. Just then, Mick appeared in the doorway and placed his arm around the woman.

"You shouldn't be answering the door," he said before shooting me a quick glance. "How about you go back to bed and I'll bring you your pills."

"My pills?" she asked.

"Yeah," he said. "And I'll get your dinner, too."

She smiled and patted his chest. "You're such a sweet boy, Mickey. Always taking care of your mother."

My eyebrows shot up. His mother. I'd expected grandma or at the very least a much older aunt, but definitely not mother. We watched in awkward silence as she hobbled up the steps one by one. When she disappeared into her room, Mick turned to me and began rubbing the back of his neck.

"She's normally not like that," he said. "It's just, she's got the flu. It makes her sorta loopy."

"It's okay," I said.

"She's really nice," he mumbled.

"I'm sure she is."

He dropped his hand and sighed. "Right, well anyway, Steve and Andy are downstairs. I'm gonna get her dinner, but then I'll be down."

As he showed me the basement door, I couldn't help but notice his face was a bright shade of red. It was almost as if he was embarrassed. Mick. *Embarrassed.* I never thought I'd see the day. I continued thinking it over while walking down the stairs. As soon as I stopped at the bottom and got a good look around, those thoughts about Mick fell to the back of my mind. There was just so damn much to take in. I mean, plain and simple, the place was a cluttered mess.

It was dimly lit with white lights strewn from the ceiling and a thick brown and orange shag carpet. Movie ads were plastered over every last inch of the walls. Everything from *The Texas Chainsaw Massacre* to *Invasion of the Body Snatchers*. There were also several concert posters and ticket stubs. *The Cramps. Haunted Garage. Rosemary's Babies. Vampire Lovers.* An old piano and a beaten up acoustic guitar leaned against the wood-paneled wall as well as a stack of dusty board games. Next to that was a bookshelf that contained a graveyard of broken toys: Rock 'em Sock 'em Robots that were missing their heads; melted and deformed G.I Joe action figures; even an Easy Bake Oven with a cracked plastic front. In the corner was a small Zenith television and a beaten up couch that seemed extremely out of place with its bright green and purple floral pattern and frilly skirt to match.

Just then, something heavy knocked into me. It wasn't long until I noticed the bright blue hair and realized it was Andy. She had her arms wrapped around me and her head pressed into my chest which caused my stomach to flutter. I wasn't sure what to do, so I remained rigid until she pulled away.

"I'm so stoked you made it," she said.

Before I could answer, Steve appeared from a back room with a beer in hand. "Ey yo, Charl-ay! You ready for some good ol' fashion teen wolf drama? It's just like the movie, only better."

"I'm ready," I said.

"Dude…" He stopped and raised his eyebrow. "You're about to witness mankind transform into a terrorizing, blood-thirsty beast and that's all you got for me? How about a hell yeah?"

I cleared my throat and let out a meager, "Hell yeah."

He laughed and shook his head. "Yo, that's weak. We're definitely gonna have to work on that."

Andy grabbed my arm and pulled me along. "Come with me. We only got half an hour until he changes. I wanna make sure you're ready."

She pulled me to the ugly couch and we sat. I noticed a torn up purple backpack covered with safety pins and patches resting on the coffee table. She reached in and pulled out a hand gun with a dark, wooden grip and long steel barrel.

"Whoa," I said, my eyes growing wide.

"This here's a Webley tranquilizer gun," she said before digging back in and pulling out a long, skinny dart with a pink feather tip. "And this is the ammo. I know it might not look like much, but a single one of these darts can take down a full grown grizzly bear. If this were to come in contact with a human, it'd be 100% lethal. That's what makes this tricky. If we shoot Mick even a second too soon, he's dead."

Steve threw himself next to her and grabbed the dart. "But shoot too late, and you're dog food."

"It's all about the timing," she said.

"Yeah, and god forbid you miss," he added.

She snatched the dart back and smirked. "Well, he doesn't have to worry about that because I don't miss."

"But what if you do?" I asked.

"She won't," Steve said. "She's got a killer shot, dude."

"He's right," she said. "But to put your mind at ease, I always pack a backup in case the first dose wears off."

"That happens?" I asked.

"Not exactly," she said. "At least, it hasn't happened yet. But I'd much rather be safe than sorry, wouldn't you?"

I heard the basement door kick open and feet pounded down the steps. Mick appeared at the base of the stairs with his arms full of junk. He shuffled toward us and dropped it all on the coffee table.

"Let's get to it," he said.

"Aye, aye, captain," Steve said as he tossed me a camo helmet. "Gear up, dude. It's time for war."

I frowned and looked at the pile of crap. There were binoculars, bandannas, t-shirts, sunglasses, and even a plastic rifle—all of it camouflage. They dove right in, tossing stuff back and forth, and before I knew it, Andy was smearing war paint on everyone's faces. We looked like a bunch of extras from the movie *Platoon*. And it didn't stop there. The next step was to turn the couch over and use it as a barricade while Mick sat cross-legged at the other side of the room. The whole thing felt absolutely ridiculous.

"And now we wait," Andy said, her eyes locked on Mick and finger on the trigger. "The actual transformation doesn't take all that long. Probably just a minute or so. The trick is to hold fire until he growls."

"Why's that?" I asked.

"It means he's truly no longer human," she said.

Steve took a swig of beer and smirked. "You know, Charlie, Mick's more jacked than Dolph Lundgren and Apollo Creed combined once he's a full-on werewolf. I bet he could rip a full grown man in half like a piece of tissue paper."

Andy rolled her eyes. "Would you quit trying to scare him?"

"I'm just being honest," he said.

"No, you're being an idiot," she snapped.

They continued back and forth, but I ignored them and looked to

Mick. He sat with his back against the wall and was messing with one of those *Tiger* handheld video games. I couldn't help but think he was awfully calm for someone about to get shot with a lethal dart. It was then that my attention was stolen by a beautiful shimmery fog seeping through the cracks in the glass of the egress window above him. I perked up.

"Hey guys," I said, pointing across the room. "Is that normal?"

"Is what normal?" Steve asked.

"That fog," I said.

"Fog?" He glanced at Andy and raised his eyebrow. "Dude, are you high? There's no fog."

"Sure there is," I said. "By the window. Don't you see it?"

Andy looked at me and furrowed her brow. "Steve's right, Charlie. There's nothing there."

I opened my mouth to argue, but then it hit me—they couldn't see it. Of course they couldn't; the fog was probably supernatural. I held my breath and whipped back around to find it circling around Mick and closing in fast. The second it touched him, his skin and lips faded to an icy shade of blue.

"This is it," Andy said, tightening her grip on the gun.

Steve downed the last bits of his beer before turning to me. "Not much left to do but sit back, relax, and enjoy the show."

I watched in awe as the fog sparkled like a thousand diamonds. It swirled in a circle, slow at first, but faster and faster until suddenly, it stopped. As it dissipated, Mick hunched over and began jerking around and grunting as if an invisible being were kicking him. Soon after, there were sounds of bones snapping and cracking as his limbs stretched and bent into grotesque shapes. I couldn't stand to watch another second and glanced at Andy who remained as still as stone, her jaw clenched with the gun held steady. Steve, on the other hand, belched and cracked open another beer.

There was a sudden ear-piercing shout that shook me to my core. I gasped and turned back, but Mick was gone. In his place was a seven-foot-tall *thing* with rippling muscles and limbs as thick as tree trunks. It stood on its hind legs and had leathery skin as well as a long pointed snout. And the teeth were like nothing I'd ever seen before— impossibly long and sharp and dripping with saliva. At first, the thing appeared dazed as it looked around the room. But as soon as it's eyes landed on us, the corner of it's lip pulled into a snarl.

"Shoot him already," Steve whispered.

"Not yet," Andy said.

She kept her eyes locked on the creature as it crept toward us like a lion stalking its prey. I didn't dare move or breathe and hoped like hell the thing couldn't hear my heart pounding. It wasn't until it opened its mouth and let out the most terrifying growl that she pulled the trigger. The dart pierced it right in the neck and immediately, it's mouth snapped shut, and it stumbled back. It whimpered and swayed back and forth until all too fast, it dropped like a sack of potatoes.

Without wasting a second, Steve leapt from behind the couch and jetted to the beast's side. He pressed his fingers against its neck and waited a moment before smiling and throwing his hands in the air.

"We got a pulse," he shouted. "He's alive!"

"Bullseye," Andy said.

She lowered her gun and rushed to give Steve a high-five, but not me; I stayed put. And not just because I was scared stiff. There was this weird feeling brewing in the pit of my stomach. One where I was both totally amped, but also needed to hurl.

After a moment, I forced myself to my feet and trudged over. For whatever reason, my mouth was too dry to form words, so I simply stared at the motionless lump that laid before me. It was just so damn bizarre being that close to a real live werewolf. Of course I'd heard my father rant about them from time to time, and a few times I actually saw one from a distance, but nothing like this.

"So what'd you think?" Andy asked.

"Yeah, dude," Steve said. "How was your first werewolf takedown?"

I had no words. In fact, I was pretty sure I was still in complete and utter shock. I lowered myself until I was face to face with the beast. With a shaky hand, I ran my fingers over it's snout. I could feel it's warm, wet breath against my skin; it was like nothing I'd ever experienced before. As terrified as I was, I couldn't help but let out a soft laugh.

"That was awesome," I said.

Steve placed his hand behind his ear and smirked. "Sorry, dude. You're gonna have to speak up."

I smiled and got back to my feet. "I said, that was *fucking* awesome!"

He slapped my back. "That's what I'm talking about! You know what? You deserve a beer, dude. You want one, Andy?"

"Sure," she said.

I hardly had time to think as he darted to the laundry room and came back with a handful of beers. I'd never drank alcohol before, but by that point I was too high on adrenaline to really be all that nervous. Steve cracked open the cans, and before I knew it, he and Andy raised their drinks.

"To new friends," Steve said.

"Yeah," Andy added. "It's official. You're one of us now,

Charlie."

"God help you," Steve muttered before turning to me with a grin. "Dude, no one knows where the hell you came from, you never fucking talk, and apparently you see ghosts. You're a total freak. But I mean that in the best of ways."

I watched as they clinked their cans and took a drink. We might've been chugging cheap beer in a dusty old basement with an unconscious werewolf at our feet, but that moment really stuck with me. I was one of them now. Their *friend*. When I finally brought that can to my lips and took my first ever sip of beer, I did it with a smile. Unfortunately, the bitter taste was not at all what I expected, and I immediately coughed it back up.

"You think that's bad," Steve said as he patted my back. "Just wait until you take your first shot."

"You brought liquor?" Andy asked.

"No," he said. "But I'm pretty sure Mick's mom's got a bottle of vodka in the liquor cabinet upstairs."

Before I knew it, he skipped up the steps and was back with a clear glass bottle and a mischievous grin. It wasn't until I took my first sip that I'd realized just why he was smirking. It was frickin' *terrible*. It took everything in me not to throw it right back up. After that, I decided no more hard liquor and opted instead to spend the rest of the night sipping beer. At least *Pabst Blue Ribbon* didn't make me feel like a hole had burned through my throat.

As the night wore on, Steve continued to make a dent in the vodka while Andy and I stuck to beer. At one point, he had us in stitches as he did impressions of the teachers around school. But then it seemed he had too much and passed out on the middle of the basement floor, the bottle still in hand. Andy took off his shoes and gave him a pillow and blanket before joining me on the couch.

At first I was kind of nervous being alone with her. After all, she was a girl, which was a species I wasn't all that familiar with. But I eased up once we started playing what she called "The Question Game" which was basically a game where we bounced back and forth and asked each other questions. After a while, my nerves went away, and I found myself really coming out of my shell. She was so easy to talk to, and I don't know why, but we just sort of clicked. Of course, the alcohol didn't hurt either.

It was well past midnight when she sprawled out on her back and rested her feet on my lap.

"All right, my question," she said. "What's your favorite book?"

"*Frankenstein*," I said without hesitation.

"Really?"

"Yeah, I always related to his character. The way he's isolated and lonely and doesn't belong anywhere. I just think he's misunderstood. I mean, it really sucks having no one like you. I don't think it's his fault that his outlook on life is so bleak; I'm the same way. I guess I just understand his frustration."

I placed my can of beer to my lips. Not to take a drink, but rather to stop the onslaught of word vomit I couldn't seem to control. I wouldn't exactly say I was drunk, at least not to Steve's standards. But for the first time in my life, I was actually having trouble keeping my mouth shut.

"Wow, that's pretty drab," she said.

"Yeah," I mumbled.

"*Frankenstein's* a great choice though. You know, back then, women had to publish their novels anonymously if they wanted anyone to read them. Because of that, a lot of people thought Mary Shelley's husband wrote the book. But no, a woman was behind one of the most iconic horror novels ever written. God, Mary Shelley was such a badass." She took a quick swig of beer and nodded to me. "Anyway, your turn, Charlie."

I looked at her black and white striped socks that rested on my lap and began to rack my brain for a question. The only problem was, I couldn't think of a single one. I must've been taking forever, because after a while, she let out a sharp laugh.

"God, you suck at this game," she said.

"Sorry."

"Nah, don't worry about it. Besides, I got about a *million* things I want to ask you. Like this whole supernatural thing."

"What about it?" I asked.

"I don't know," she said. "Tell me something crazy and dark that you've never told anyone before."

"I already told you guys everything I know."

She prodded my chest with her foot. "That's bullshit. I bet you know way more than you let on."

"I really don't."

"Come *on*," she said, rolling her eyes. "There has to be something you've failed to mention."

"There's not—"

She dug her foot into my side and smirked. "You're a liar, Charlie. A dirty rotten liar, and a terrible one at that."

I attempted to hold back a smile and wrestle away from her, but she poked me harder and harder, not letting up until finally, her big toe pressed into the nape of my neck, and I let loose a laugh.

"Fine," I said. "It's not a big deal, but I guess this one time I snuck a look through my dad's stuff."

"Look at you, rebel." She took a sip of beer and winked. "Well, then. Go on, James Dean."

"What?"

"Give me the details!"

"Right…"

I sighed and rubbed my hands over my face as I thought back to that day. I was thirteen or so and living in some small town I forgot the name of because by that point in my life, all those crap hole trailer parks blended together. Ever since I could remember, there was this old book my father was obsessed with. It was thick and leather bound and held together by a brass lock. I wasn't allowed anywhere near it, so when the day finally came where I found it not only unlocked, but spread open on my father's bedside table, I couldn't help myself and just had to look through it.

"It was filled with these weird handwritten notes and sketches," I said. "I'm not sure if it was based on anything factual or if it was total fantasy, but the drawings were graphic. Like, really disturbing stuff. Lots of human sacrifice and dismemberment. Then there were these horsemen or whatever that all represented something different. Darkness, war, disease, and virtue I think it was."

"Like in the bible?" she asked.

"The bible?"

"Yeah, the four horsemen of the apocalypse. I think it was in the new testament."

"How'd you know that?"

"I'm Latina," she said with a smirk. "I grew up super catholic. Anyway, they're supposed to signify the end of the world. It sounds like maybe your dad's book was just a knock off of that."

"Maybe," I said. "But it didn't really seem all that religious. It kind of read like a cook book or something."

"A *cook book*?"

"Okay, maybe not exactly. I just meant that it sort of read like instructions, or a manual or something. I don't know how to describe it."

"Well, what did it say?"

"I'm not sure. I didn't get to read much further before I got caught."

"Ouch," she said. "Did your dad flip?"

I felt a hitch in my stomach and began fidgeting with the ends of my shirt. The truth was, he beat me within an inch of my life, but that wasn't exactly something I wanted to share with her or anyone really. I felt her eyes bearing into me as we sat in silence until finally she let out a soft laugh.

"You know, this is the most I've ever heard you talk," she said.

"Sorry."

"*Sorry*? Come on, Charlie."

"What?"

"This is, like, the fifth time you've apologized tonight. Never apologize." She moved her feet from my lap and sat up. "Anyway, it's your turn. And this time, I'm not letting you off easy. You got to think of something good."

I bit down on my lip and focused. A question. A simple question. Something I wanted to know. *Anything*. God, why couldn't I think of something? In my defense, it was kind of hard when I had her staring at me the entire time. It was then my mind flashed to earlier in the evening and the words just sort of fell out.

"Is Mick's mom all right?" I asked.

"What do you mean?"

"I don't know, it just kind of seems like she's sick or something."

"Right…" She rubbed her forehead. "Well, it's kind of a sad story actually. Back when Mick was thirteen or so she got a bad head injury and hasn't been the same since." She paused and furrowed her brow. "Has Mick ever mentioned his dad to you before?"

"Sort of," I said.

"What'd he say exactly?"

"Not much. He just told me he was a prick."

"Yeah," she said, rolling her eyes. "That's an understatement. He treated Mick and his mom like total crap. It was mostly verbal abuse, but this one time he took it too far. Long story short, Mick's dad caught him with another guy."

"Another guy?"

"Yeah," she said.

"Doing what?"

She smirked. "You know.. "

"I, uh….." I rubbed the back of my neck. "I'm not sure I do."

"Charlie, come *on*." She let out a soft laugh. "Mick's gay."

"He's *what*?"

"Gay," she said again. "You know, I'm honestly not all that surprised he didn't tell you. He used to be totally open about it but not so much anymore. Not since his dad caught him kissing a boy and… well, he started kicking the crap out of him. Mick's mom stepped in to protect him and ended up getting the brunt of it."

"That's horrible," I said.

"Yeah, it is. Ever since then, Mick's sort of been uncomfortable about who he is. It's like he thinks being gay is what hurt his mom or something. It doesn't matter how many times I tell him it wasn't his fault; he won't believe me."

"But that's not right."

"It's just the way it is, Charlie. You can't force people to see the truth when they're already buried so deep in self-hatred." For a moment, she stared at me before she glanced at the clock on the wall and let out a breath. "Anyway, it's getting late. We should probably try to get some sleep."

She gave my hand a squeeze and hopped to her feet to switch the light off. As she grabbed a blanket and curled up at the other end of the couch, I got comfortable on the lazy boy across from her.

"Night, Charlie," she said.

"Night," I replied.

For the longest time, I laid in the darkness and thought about Mick. I just couldn't get my mind off of him. It made me so damn angry. I couldn't wrap my mind around the fact that someone wanted to hurt him. I mean, this was *Mick.* The same guy who was always dancing or laughing and acted like an excited puppy. He didn't deserve it. No one deserved that sort of abuse.

It was then that a daunting thought crossed my mind and sent a chill down my spine. I pulled the covers to my chin and tried to ignore it, but it was there, scratching away at the back of my mind like always.

No one deserved that sort of abuse.

Except maybe me.

We waited until Mick woke up the next morning and checked to make sure he was okay. As he put it, the mornings after getting tranquilized were like a hangover from hell; he wanted nothing more than to pound some Gatorade and go back to sleep. We got him settled in his bed and said our goodbyes before walking home.

After parting ways with the others, I popped in the cassette Andy had leant me. It was this album called *Hysterie* by *Teenage Jesus and the Jerks*. Apparently the lead singer, Lydia Lunch, was one of her idols. The band was very experimental and used a lot of unique sounds. This one song in particular stuck with me. *Little girl in your little girl world, dressed in baby gowns in your baby doll town, watch me baby walk watch me baby talk. I'm a little girl in your little girl world.*

I was so lost in the music that when I walked through the back door to Aunt Joy's place, I hardly noticed the small chocolate cake sitting on the kitchen table. Before I knew it, Aunt Joy had her arms wrapped around me and was swinging me back and forth. I slipped off my headphones to hear her singing an overly dramatic rendition of *Happy Birthday*. When she was done, she kissed the side of my head and looked me over with a smile.

"Happy birthday, Charlie," she said. "Gosh, I can't believe you're already eighteen years old!"

"Huh?"

"It's your birthday," she said. "Don't tell me you forgot?"

"Oh," I mumbled and rubbed the back of my neck. "I guess I did."

"Don't worry, sweetheart. Lucky for you, I never forget a birthday." She brushed the hair from my face and sighed.

"Unfortunately, I have to head to work early tonight, but I thought maybe we could do the whole cake and candles thing now, then really celebrate tomorrow. How does that sound?"

I nodded.

"Wonderful," she said as she patted her pockets. "Now, where'd I put that damned lighter?"

As she scavenged through the drawers, I slowly lowered myself onto a chair at the table and stared at the cake with a dazed expression. With all that'd been going on, I completely forgot about my birthday. Not that I would've given it much thought if I *had* remembered; I never celebrated my birthday, and I most definitely never got a cake. When she finally joined me at the table, she lit the candles and pushed the dessert in front of me.

"You know," she said. "I still remember when Nadine turned eighteen. It feels like just yesterday that our mother and I baked her that double decker, cream cheese icing and strawberry cake."

I perked up.

"Her eighteenth birthday," she said longingly. "Did your father ever tell you that story?"

By this point, my heart was beating in my throat. Nadine was my mother. And no, my father never told me that story. He never told me *any* stories. The only reason I even knew her name was because I once found a crinkled up picture of her hidden in his sock drawer that had her name written on the back.

"He never told me," I finally managed to choke out.

"No?"

I shook my head.

She looked at the cake and grinned. "Well, it's such a cute story. You see, your father was madly in love with Nadine from the moment he laid eyes on her. For years, he chased after her, but she turned him down time and time again. Your mother would never admit to this, but it was obvious she loved being chased just as much as Allan seemed to love hearing her say no. For far too long, I had to put up with her ranting about Allan this, or Allan that, but whenever she said his name, she always had a hint of a smile. Gosh, I'll never forget that smile. It was the strangest game only they seemed to understand, but I have no doubt in my mind they loved every second of it."

As she spoke, I kept my jaw clenched and glared at the table. On the one hand, I wanted her to stop talking because I couldn't stand to hear another word about my father. But at the same time, I was desperate to learn more about my mom. Just hearing her name was enough to keep me silent.

"Anyway," she said, "the months leading up to Nadine's eighteenth birthday, Allan begged her to let him take her on a date. She finally agreed to go out with him, but on one condition: he had to sing to her in front of the entire school. Now, it was a well-known fact that Allan couldn't carry a tune to save his life, so never in her wildest dreams did she think he'd actually go through with it. But of course he did. He would do absolutely anything for her. And that very afternoon, he interrupted a school assembly to serenade her in front of the entire class." She closed her eyes and began to sing. "*Come softly, darling. Come to me, stay. You're my obsession. Forever and a day.*"

My entire body jolted. It caused my chair to scrape loudly against the tile floor. That song. I hated that song. Aunt Joy immediately stopped singing and looked at me with a worried expression.

"Everything all right, dear?" she asked.

"I'm fine."

"You sure?"

"Yeah, it's just…" I clenched my jaw. "I really don't like that song."

She stared at me in an uncomfortable silence, but I refused to look at her. I just couldn't bring myself to do it because I knew exactly what she was thinking. After a while, she placed her hand on mine.

"I'm so sorry, honey," she said softly. "I know your relationship with your father hasn't been all that strong, especially as of late. But you have to know he wasn't always bad. He had a tough life. When he was just fourteen, he ran away from home and was living in an old janitor's closet at our school. My father used to teach his English class and when he found Allan, he took him in that very day. He became a part of our family. In fact, he's like a brother to me. And he didn't speak of it all that much, but we all knew the reason he ran away was because of the abuse from his father."

"I'm not surprised," I snapped.

"How do you mean?"

"He had to learn it from somewhere, didn't he?"

As soon as the words left my mouth, I regretted them. Not because they weren't true, but because I could tell it crushed my aunt to hear. Her eyes immediately began to well with tears.

"I didn't mean that," I said quickly.

"It's all right."

"No, really. I'm sorry."

"Don't be, honey. You're right. What Allan did to you was absolutely unforgivable, and I'm sorry for making excuses for him. I just wish you could have known him as I did. Gosh, he was just so charming and charismatic. Handsome, too. He had a real way with words. Everyone loved him. And he loved your mother, Charlie. Oh, he loved her with all his heart, I have no doubt about that. I swear, the way he looked at her was so full of love. He would do anything for her."

I kept my mouth shut because I didn't want to upset her again, but the truth was, I hated my father. The man I knew was a miserable, violent, asshole with a short fuse. I'd never forgive him.

She wiped her tears and smiled. "But enough about that, sweetheart. It's your birthday. Let's celebrate. How about you blow out your candles and make a wish?"

Without thinking, I closed my eyes and blew out the candles while wishing for the one thing any sane teenager would—my father to drop dead. The smoke drifted from the tips of the extinguished candles and disappeared into nothingness. At the same time, a terrible rage began to brew in the pit of my stomach. My aunt didn't seem to notice and went on to talk about something or another while she cut the cake, but I couldn't hear her. I was somewhere else, lost in a distant memory. And with each passing second, that memory grew more intense. It was something I'd tried so damn hard to lock away but now it broke free and was fighting its way to the front of my mind, demanding to be heard.

I wasn't sure how much time had passed because everything was a blur. At some point my aunt had disappeared upstairs to get ready for work while I remained in the kitchen and stared at the cake. Just stared. No movement. I was numb as I studied every last inch of that yellow bread with its dark chocolate frosting as if it held all the answers to the universe. And then my aunt kissed the top of my head. There was the slam of a door. The sound of an engine. The second the car left the driveway, something in me snapped. It was like a firework had gone off inside me. I screamed a sweet release of pent up rage and smacked the plate with the back of my hand. It went crashing into the wall and immediately shattered, the cake crumbling to bits.

I shot to my feet and my chair toppled over, but I didn't care. I had to get out of there. I marched to my room with the hope that lying on my bed might calm me down. It didn't. I tried taking long, deep breaths, but there just wasn't enough air. It felt as though an invisible fist had wrapped around my heart and was squeezing it into submission. I was suffocating. It was then my mind drifted to the smell of cheap Irish whiskey; the pain in my side; the sound of a record scratching on a turntable.

That song.

I hated that fucking song. *Come softly, darling. Come to me, stay. You're my obsession. Forever and a day.*

I dragged my hands over my face, but that memory still clawed at the back of my head, scratching and scraping until I couldn't hide from it any more. That song. It'd been playing that night. My father screamed over it while he paced back and forth in the kitchen. The sounds of his boots echoed off the tiles. *Radar, radar. Charlie, he's coming!* He was ranting about that stupid book. He lost it or someone stole it or something. I wasn't sure because I was doing my best to tune him out. I was tucked in the back of the closet just as I'd always been, my head in my hands as I tried to pretend I was somewhere else. There was an overpowering stench of smoke and whiskey. It was so strong, I had to bury my nose in my shirt.

The next thing I remembered was glass shattering and footsteps. The floor shook. The closet door flung open. Standing in front of me was my father, in his hand a jagged shard of glass. He squeezed it until his fist trembled and blood trickled to the beige carpet below him. That was when it clicked. This wasn't like all those other times. He wouldn't just take his anger out on me and then pass out in a drunken stupor. No.

This was it. The end. He was going to kill me. Kill *us*.

It was strange to stare death in the face. I always thought when the moment came, I'd just lie down and take it, but I'm surprised to say I didn't. I was a fighter. With every last bit of strength I could summon, I threw my body at him and attempted to knock him over. He grabbed my arm and yanked me back, in the process slicing a deep gash on my cheek bone. Before I knew it, I was pinned against the wall with his bloody hand wrapped around my throat. His face was inches from mine, his whiskey breath invading my nostrils as I struggled to breath. I'd never forget the look in his eye. He wasn't angry. He wasn't crazed. It was the look of a pathetic old man who'd simply given up.

He whimpered something that sounded like an apology, but it wasn't me he was talking to; that much was clear. He might've been looking me dead in the eye, but it was her name he sobbed over and over. Nadine. He told her how much he loved her, how he tried his hardest, how he *really* tried. The last words he said were, "I'll see you soon," before he thrust the shard of glass into my side. I screamed as it dug deeper, twisting, sending an explosion of fire through my entire body. When he finally let go of my throat, it was as if all the strength had been sapped from me, and I collapsed in a heap on the floor. I clutched my stomach, screaming in agony as I felt the shard of glass still lodged in me. I didn't dare move it. I didn't dare move at all. All I could do was just wait to die as the edges of my vision darkened.

I wasn't in my trailer.

I was in my room.

I was safe.

No matter how many times I repeated those words, the imaginary fist continued to squeeze my heart. It was a panic attack; that much I knew for sure. But this wasn't like any panic attack I'd ever experienced before. Instead of fear, I felt anger. Pure unadulterated anger. And as I leapt to my feet and began to pace back and forth, that anger grew stronger. I hated my father. I hated what he did to me. Even worse, I hated that I let it happen. I let it fucking happen. All those years I spent letting him knock me around. That was my fault. I could've stood up to him. I could've run away. I could've done *something*. But I didn't. I did nothing.

Blind fury ate through me like a virus. It started in my stomach but soon spread to the very ends of my fingers and toes before bubbling to my throat until it erupted like a volcano and I screamed. I screamed long and hard. I just wanted all that anger gone. Out of me. It was a poison I had to cleanse myself of. I clenched my fists and screamed until my head hurt and my throat grew coarse, and then I took a breath and screamed some more. When that wasn't enough, I drove my fist through the wall. I heard something crack and pain shot up my arm, but I didn't care. In fact, I liked the pain; it was a channel through which my anger could finally escape. I punched the wall again and again until it was splattered with blood. When I finally stopped, my entire body was shaking. It was horrible, but at the same time wonderful. It was cathartic. Relief. I needed more.

It was then I noticed my Springsteen cassette resting on my bedside table. I thought back to all those times I spent curled up in my closet while I listened to it. Those songs were prison. They stood for everything I used to be. Weak. Pathetic. I would *never* go back to the way things were. Without thinking, I snatched it from the table and chucked it to the floor before driving my heel through it. The sound of plastic cracking was euphoric. I did it again and again until it was broken into a million little pieces.

When I was finally done, I collapsed onto my bed and breathed a sigh of relief. Even though my shirt was drenched in sweat, and my knuckles were bloodied, at least I could breathe again. And the more air I inhaled, the better I felt. For the first time in my life, I released the anguish that'd been without a doubt killing me the past eighteen years. It was amazing, almost as though I was an entirely new person. A stronger person. In that moment, the whole world was at my feet.

I was free.

It was a Friday morning in October when I found a poorly cut out newspaper article taped to my locker. *Loudon County Crops Dying at Worrisome Rate,* the headline read. I checked over my shoulder, confused as to who would do this. It wasn't until I heard Scotty's voice that it all started to make sense.

"Strange, isn't it?" he asked.

I pinched the bridge of my nose and groaned. That morning he opted to wear a red bandanna tied across his forehead and knotted at the side. He paired it with green army pants and chunky black boots that had me convinced that he might've watched the movie *Rambo* one too many times.

"You gotta be kidding me," I mumbled.

"It's lovely seeing you, too," he said sarcastically.

"What do you want?"

"What do I *want*?" His hands shot to his hips. "In this past month alone, Ashburn has reported more than fifty acres of wheat to be completely decayed. And then there was a dairy farmer in Leesburg who claimed his entire stock of twenty plus cows just up and died out of nowhere. In Sterling there's talks about an unknown disease eating away at all of their corn stalks. In Stone Ridge—"

"Get to the point," I snapped.

"Apparently there's some unknown disease floating around the county."

"Okay."

"*Okay*? That's all you have to say?"

"I mean, it's sad and all, but what does it have to do with me?"

"Everything! Wake up, Charlie! I mean, Christ on earth, what else has to happen for you to get it through your thick skull that this is clearly some sort of supernatural phenomenon at play?"

I rolled my eyes. "I'm gonna say this one last time. This, whatever *this* is, has nothing to do with me or even you for that matter. You can do whatever the hell you want, but just leave me out of it, all right?"

"No can do," he said.

"Why not?"

"I already told you. I need you. You're a Venator. I've been waiting for years to come across one of your kind, and now that I have, I'm not letting you go no matter how stubborn and boneheaded you might be."

"I'm not a Venator," I said.

"Yes, you—"

"No. I'm a teenager. And I just wanna go to school in peace. Is that really too much to ask?"

I turned my back to him and began fiddling with my locker combination in the hopes that he'd leave me alone, but I should've known better. He forced himself next to me and was back in my ear.

"What about the suicides?" he asked.

"God, are you still on about that?"

"Just shut up and listen," he said. "On the day of the fire, twenty-four people perished in the flames while an additional six victims were reported in critical condition and taken to the hospital. Within the next week, there were exactly *twenty-four* supposedly unrelated suicides. As for the six people in critical condition, five of them have passed, each one followed by an unexplained and totally bizarre suicide within hours. Even you have to admit, that's very strange."

I remained silent and stared at my shoes. He wasn't wrong, but I didn't want to tell him that. After a long pause, he leaned close to my ear and lowered his voice, sending chills down my spine.

"There's one left," he said. "Good ol' Aryeh Azriel, the town Rabbi. He's in the hospital and last I checked, he ain't doing too hot. I bet once he finally bites the bullet, it won't be long until someone follows in his footsteps. What do you think?"

I slammed my locker in his face. "I think I have to get to class."

His brow lowered. "Are you kidding me? *Class*?"

"Yeah, we're in school after all."

"Screw class! We need to come up with a plan."

"Like what?"

"I don't know, but anything's better than pretending the world's all hunky dory while gallivanting around town with Johnny Rotten and the gang."

"Just give it a rest already," I said as I brushed past him.

"Where are you going?" he called after me.

"I told you, class."

He raised his voice. "Aryeh Azriel is gonna croak, Charlie! And once he does, you're gonna come crawling right back to me, just you wait!"

A few people turned to stare, but I ignored them and continued down the hall. I had convinced myself at this point that Scotty was grasping at straws. He had to be. There was no dark magic or evil curses; he was just being paranoid. Besides, I had more important things to worry about. For example, going to see the *Swiz* show that evening. They were this new punk band Steve had been obsessing over nonstop for the past few weeks. That night, they had a concert up in the city and tickets were just five bucks, so we all decided we'd hop on a train after school to see them play.

Before the concert, we decided to grab a quick bite to eat at *The Guillotine*. We sat in our booth near the back where I picked at a plate of fries and listened as my friends gushed about the upcoming show. They were dressed to the nines, which kind of made me feel lame in my lackluster flannel and blue jeans. Andy had on a pair of leather pants and wore a heavy black liner around her eyes. Steve on the other hand supported a jean jacket that was covered in spikes and studs, while Mick had on a ridiculous looking pair of red plaid pants that had all sorts of weird belts and zippers attached to it. Toward the end of our meal, Mick dug out a wadded up t-shirt from his backpack and threw it at me.

"What's this?" I asked.

"It's a shirt," he said. "Wear it. You're gonna sweat your balls off in that thick ass flannel."

I laughed a little as I unfolded the shirt which featured this band called *The Cramps* and a picture of what looked like a human fly. There were sharpie scribblings covering every last inch of white space, which I was certain Mick had done by hand. After a moment, I lowered the shirt and frowned.

"I thought we were going to see *Swiz*," I said.

"We are," Mick replied.

"So then, why'd you give me a *Cramps* shirt?" I asked.

Steve began choking on his soda. "Dude, no. Just *no*," he said between coughs. "Tell me you're not serious?"

"About what?" I asked.

"*Dude!*" He pounded his fist on the table. "Didn't anyone ever tell you? *Never* wear a band shirt for the band you're actually going to see. That's like, sacreligious or whatever. It's punishable by death!"

"You're overreacting," Andy said.

"Tell that to Ray." He turned to me, his eyes wide. "This one time, my brother Ray went to a *Dag Nasty* concert wearing one of their shirts, and when he came home, he had a bloody nose and broken arm."

"Bullshit," Andy said.

"It's *true*," Steve insisted.

She rolled her eyes. "Ray's a total jerk off. I bet he got his ass kicked for being a douchebag, not for wearing a stupid shirt. Besides, it's a totally mental rule. No one at a punk show actually gives a crap what you're wearing. At least not the people that matter."

"It's not a dumb rule," Steve said. "If you—"

"Can we just focus?" Mick interrupted before nodding to me. "Charlie, man, that right there's my all-time favorite shirt. Got it at my first ever concert. You wear that, and you'll fit right in. Promise."

"Wow," I said, holding it closer. "Thanks."

"No problem." He checked his watch. "Anyway, we should probably head out soon. We don't wanna miss the train."

"Wait," Andy said as she reached into her purple backpack. "One last thing before we go."

I was worried she'd pull out a spiked collar or a razor blade bracelet or something else totally outlandish to go with my shirt, but to my surprise, she pulled out a bright blue sharpie marker.

"What's that for?" I asked.

"It's for you," Andy said, handing it to me. "We want you to sign your name next to ours."

"Yeah," Steve added. "Right under the guillotine. Best place in the house."

My jaw dropped and I gawked at the marker as if it were some foreign tool from another planet. Andy thrust it in my hands and it snapped me out of my daze. Before I knew it, I was yanked up and out of my seat and was kneeling before the guillotine as if it were some holy shrine with its dark, rustic wood and iron hinges, not to mention the way the light reflected off my friend's scribbled names made them seem so important. With a deep breath, I uncapped the marker and signed my name right next to theirs. It was nervous with everyone staring at me, so the letters were sort of shaky, but there it was in big bold letters: *Charlie Stewart.*

"It's official," Mick said.

"Yeah," Steve added. "And it's a permanent marker, so there ain't no getting rid of us now."

I laughed at that, because I couldn't imagine wanting to get rid of them. If anything, I figured it'd be the other way around. When I got to my feet, they began to cheer way too loud and slapped my back. It was so over the top, everyone in the restaurant turned to stare, but I didn't care. It was just us. Me and my friends against the world. Screw what everyone else thought.

On our way to the train station, we decided to take a quick detour to the convenience store for snacks. It was one of those old, rinky dink quick stops that sold scratch off lottery tickets and nasty slow roasted hot dogs that probably weren't fit for human consumption. The windows were caged in with metal bars and the shelves were covered in dust. The guy working the front register hardly paid us any attention as we walked in. He had his feet kicked up on the counter as he flipped through an issue of *Mad Magazine*. I wasn't really all that hungry since we'd just ate, but Steve wasted no time and darted straight to the junk food aisle like a kid in a candy shop. He immediately grabbed several bags of *Ruffles* and *Slim Jims* while Mick hit up the candy section. Andy went to the restroom, so I found myself alone, wandering through the refrigerated aisle while I waited for my friends.

I must've looked suspicious or something because the cashier kept peeking at me from behind his magazine. He was an older guy with a grease stained shirt and a fat beer gut. I flashed him an awkward smile and did my best to ignore him as I walked past the malt liquor and over to the corner where there apparently was a buy one get one half off deal for two six packs of *Squeezits*.

It was then that I heard a bell and the door at the front of the shop swung open. At first, I didn't pay any attention to it and went about my business. It wasn't until a faint breeze trickled across my skin that I perked up. It was so gentle, it caused my hair to stand on end and a chill to crawl down my spine. It was followed by an eerily familiar whisper that sent a sense of dread to the pit of my stomach.

That whisper. I'd heard it before.

The cheap neon signs hanging in the front window began to flicker and buzz until they burned out. At the same time, a man walked into the shop. With him was a cloud of thick black smoke that wafted from his skin and swirled at his feet. He was hunched over, his legs bowed out so far they appeared broken. His skin was a displeasing shade of gray and sagging as if it were rotting away before my eyes, and his mouth was foaming. He wore a hospital gown that'd been shredded to pieces and covered in soot as well as a charred white scarf around his neck. I heard Scotty's voice in the back of my mind.

Good ol' Aryeh Azriel.

I'd seen a few ghosts in my time, but never once did I feel the overwhelming sense of hostility that irradiated from this one. The guy was pissed off beyond belief, and I had no doubt he wanted to cause me harm. As he hobbled into the store, his body jerked and twisted with each step. I gasped and dove behind a shelf. The light bulb above me continued to flicker as I pressed my back against a stack of *Campell's* chicken noodle soup and strained my ears for sounds of movement. It was hard to hear with the loud whispers reverberating through the entire store, but I was finally able to make out the indiscernible sound of feet dragging. It was slow and daunting, getting closer and closer with each passing second. I closed my eyes, a bead of sweat rolling down my face. Out of fear, I snatched the closest thing to me which was a pathetic can of *SpaghettiOs*. Just as I raised it up to strike, a sudden voice caused me to yelp and shoot to my feet.

It was Steve and Mick. They looked at me, their eyebrows raised.

"Whoa, there," Mick said.

"Dude, why the hell are you on the floor?" Steve asked. "And what's with the *SpaghettiOs*?"

I ignored them and spun back around. As soon as I did, my heart leapt from my chest. Aryeh Azriel. There he was, not even five feet from me; the only thing between us was a metal partition. I gasped and stumbled back, dropping the can of *SpaghettiOs*. I could see every crack in his dry lips; every blue and red vein bulging in his neck. He reeked of burned flesh and singed hair. I stared into his yellow eyes for what seemed like an eternity until suddenly, a man popped up from behind the shelves and stood between us. This one was alive and seemed normal enough with his *Boston Red Sox* cap and a jean jacket. It was alarming just how casually he examined a box of *Smurf Berry Crunch*, but then again, he was clearly unaware of the ghost standing right behind him. Before I could yell for him to run, the ghost snatched his shoulder. A cloud of black smoke forced its way into the man's mouth, nose, and eyes until his body went rigid. He convulsed violently for a few seconds, and when all was said and done, he dropped the box of cereal and made a break for the checkout counter.

"What's up with that guy?" Mick asked.

"Yeah," Steve added. "Whatever drugs he's on, I want some."

I ignored them because by that point, the whispers were stabbing at my ear drums. I covered my ears and watched helplessly as the man who'd been possessed ripped the magazine from the cashier's hands and decked him. While the cashier hunched over and clutched his face, the man clawed for something behind the counter. I wasn't sure just what it was that he wanted so bad until he pulled out a small black pistol. He was enamored with it, running his fingers over every last inch of metal. He then placed the barrel in his mouth, his lip curling as he bit down. Mick and Steve shouted as they ducked and covered, but not me. I watched in horror as the man squeezed the trigger, an explosion of blood splattering over a nice display of *Twinkies* behind him.

It wasn't until his body hit the ground that the whispers finally stopped.

Side *Two*

The Midtowne trailer park was just like all the other trailer parks I'd ever been to. It had that familiar stench of cigarettes and gasoline and was plagued by the sounds of distant highway traffic. It was also where Scotty lived, and after witnessing the demon possession or ghost attack or whatever the hell that took place at the convenience store, I knew I had to find him, stat. My friends followed, though they were obviously confused. They hurled question after question at me, but I didn't know how to answer since I barely had a grasp on things myself.

We walked past the rickety iron gate at the front of the park, and I began to pace up and down the gravel path. I was unsure how I was actually going to find his trailer; there were so damn many, and he never gave me a house number. It also didn't help that it was already dark out and the only light source was from the dusty old street lamps that lined the path. After a while, Mick finally grabbed my arm and forced me to stop.

"Charlie, man," he said. "What the hell is going on?"

"I'm looking for someone," I answered.

"Who?" he asked.

"Scotty," I said. "We need his help."

"You're freaking me out," Andy said. "Why'd you bring us here?"

I pinched the bridge of my nose and drew a deep breath. It was then that a slate gray trailer parked beneath a willow tree caught my eye. It had red symbols spray painted like hieroglyphics all along the siding. They were the same ones my father had carved into our walls. I also noticed a collection of twenty or so wooden crucifixes staked into the ground like a picket fence; this had to be it. I walked toward it like a moth drawn to a flame. My friends called after me, but I ignored them and approached the blood red front door where a garlic necklace hung like a wreath. Without wasting a second, I knocked.

Mick grabbed my shoulder and spun me around. "Seriously, man. What are you doing?"

"Just trust me," I said.

"Do you even know who lives here?" Andy asked.

"I do," I said. "And he can help us."

"With *what*?" she asked.

"It's just...." I rubbed my hands over my face. "I saw something weird, okay?"

"Yeah," Steve said. "We all saw something weird. A dude just blew his brains all over a stack of *Hostess* fucking cupcakes. That don't explain why you brought us to the white trash Amityville Horror house."

I sighed. "It'll make sense soon enough. I just—"

Before I could finish, the front door swung open and I stumbled back, nearly tripping over one of the crucifixes staked in the ground. When I looked up, the wrong end of a crossbow was thrust in my face.

"Don't shoot!" Mick shrieked.

"Yeah," Steve said. "We come in peace!"

"The sign says no solicitors," Scotty growled as he adjusted his grip on the weapon. He squinted in the darkness and when he realized it was me, he lowered the bow. "Charlie? What're you doing here?"

"I need your help," I said, my hands still held up in defense. "Aryeh Azriel. I saw his ghost."

"You what?" he asked.

"Saw his ghost," I said again. "He possessed a guy. Shot himself in the head. Suicide. You were right."

His mouth snapped shut, and he straightened. As he looked at me, I held my breath, waiting for him to say something. Anything. After a while, the corner of his lip curled ever so slightly.

"This is interesting," he said.

"What is?" I asked.

"The fact that you are here," he answered. "You know, if my memory serves me correct, I recall just this morning, I had warned you that this would happen. But you wouldn't listen to me. In fact, you absolutely *refused* to hear a word of it. Now here you are, beseeching my help like the pathetic worm that you are."

"Oh, cut me a break," I said.

"Why should I?" he asked. "You certainly didn't cut me one."

"Yeah, but...." I huffed and looked to the ground. "Come on, Scotty. This is important. I need you."

He rubbed his hands together and grinned. "Of course you do. But first, I want to hear you beg."

"Seriously?" I asked.

"I'm always serious," he said.

Steve glanced from Scotty to me before raising his eyebrow. "Yo, Charlie, who the hell is this clown?"

"Excuse me?" Scotty said, his head snapping to him. *"Clown?* I'll have you know by the time I was just thirteen-years-old, I'd already played a key role in over a hundred different demonic possessions, some of which were classified as a level three possession. I have enough 9mm ammo and rock salt stocked up to last a third world war. Not to mention, I am an expert archer and am a black belt in Shotokan. So, take this as a warning, punk. You don't want to mess with me."

Steve blinked. "Come again?"

I stepped between them and faced Scotty. "Can we just focus? I'm sorry. You were right. I was wrong. I'm a total idiot and should've listened to you from the start. Now can you please help us?"

He lifted his chin and looked down upon me with the most arrogant smile I'd ever seen. It made my skin crawl, but the truth was, we needed him. And to be fair, I *had* been acting like a total asshole the past few weeks, so I guess I deserved it. After a moment, he finally let out a haughty laugh and stepped aside.

"Come in," he said.

"Really?"

"Yes," he said. "Just don't touch anything."

I sighed in relief. "Thank you."

I rushed inside his trailer, but that relief soon turned to shock once I got a good look around. The place was a similar layout to the trailer I grew up in—a small kitchenette on one side with a row of seating on the other. In the back was what looked like a bedroom and bathroom, and the rest of the space was wooden drawers and cabinets for storage. The main difference, however, was the amount of *junk* he had. There were tons of old, dusty books stacked high and blocking any chance of light from getting in. Then of course there were newspaper clippings taped to the wall that'd detailed every last suicide from the past few weeks as well as a set of hunting knives splayed out on the kitchen counter. There were a few gallon jugs next to his sink that were labelled with black marker. One read *Catholic Holy Water,* the other two *Lutheran* and *Protestant.* Next to those was a weird purple plant that had what looked like teeth, and on his windowsill was a collection of various colored vials and glass cylinders that contained mysterious gases.

Mick and Andy whispered as they stared wide eyed at a bear trap resting on the stove, while Steve gawked at a neon green and orange water gun that'd been mounted to the wall like a prized fish. He reached out to touch it, but before he could even come close, Scotty smacked his hand away.

"That's not a toy," he snapped.

"Dude," Steve said. "That's a *Super Soaker*. It's the literal definition of a toy."

He let out a haughty laugh. "Oh yeah? Well, I'll have you know that *toy* saved me from a pack of wild Evarcha Culicivora while I was hunting along the Pacific Crest Trail a few years back."

"Evarcha Culi-*what*?" Steve asked.

"Culicivora," Scotty said. "It's a nasty breed of vampire that's typically found on the west coast. They derive many of their characteristics from spiders such as spinning their victims in a web and have fangs that inject venom."

Mick frowned. "I ain't never heard of no spider vampires before."

"That's because this isn't *Nosferatu*," Scotty sneered. "The definition of a vampire is a creature that survives off blood. Sure, some breeds of vampire look like the classics, but the Evarcha Culicivora have the torso and arms of a man and are covered in flesh. They also have eight legs and beady black eyes. Most vampires on the west coast are relatively feral as compared to the ones on the east coast." He glanced at his water gun and chuckled. "But east coast, west coast—it doesn't really matter. No vampire can stand a blast of holy water to the face."

"Whoa," Mick said, his eyes wide in astonishment. "That's some real *Kingdom of Spiders* shit."

"Totally gnarly," Steve added.

"Gnarly, yes." Scotty cleared the books and weapons from the living room chairs and gestured for us to sit. "So, Charlie. Let's get down to business. Tell me everything you saw today."

"Right," I said.

I lowered myself next to him and took a deep breath before telling him all about the whispers and the chill that filled the air as soon as the spirit walked into the convenience store; the way his body was bent and broken; his decayed skin and foaming mouth; the cloud of thick black smoke. I explained how desperate the man seemed to be to get ahold of that gun, not to mention the creepy smile that spread across his face just before he pulled the trigger. When all was said and done, I realized I was shaking.

"I might not know much," I said, "but I've definitely never seen a ghost act like that before."

"That's because we're not dealing with a ghost," Scotty said.

"We're not?" I asked.

"No," he said. "Based on the testimony you just gave, I'm confident we've come across a nasty herd of Dybbuk. I've been speculating on that possibility for a while now, but couldn't be sure until now."

"A Dybbuk?" Andy asked. "What the heck is that?"

"They're very rare," Scotty explained. "I'm not surprised you haven't heard of them. Not many have. They're from Hebrew folklore and are considered to be the dislocated souls of the dead. It takes a lot of black magic to conjure them." He paused, his expression somber. "A lot of black magic and murder."

"The fire," I whispered.

"Exactly," he said. "Someone started that fire on purpose and used black magic to capture the souls of those who perished. What ends up happening is the spirits get so confused and angry that they're tethered to earth. The longer they're stuck here, the angrier they get until they go rabid. They find a body to possess in order to kill themselves so they can finally move on to the afterlife."

"That's horrible," Andy said.

"Yes, it is," Scotty replied. "But I suspect the Dybbuk are just the beginning. If you haven't noticed, every single day since the fire, Midtwone has been shrouded in darkness. That's no coincidence. On top of that, there has been an outbreak of disease that's been killing all the local crops and livestock. I can't figure out exactly how everything is connected, but my gut tells me it is." He turned to me and glared. "And as Charlie has recently discovered, my gut is always right."

"So, let me get this straight," Steve said. "All these recent suicides are because of a bunch of pissed off ghosts?"

"In a sense," Scotty said.

"Fucking 'A, dude," he said. "How the hell do you even know all this? Are you one of those Venator things, too?"

Scotty's shoulders deflated. "I am not. Though I'd still consider myself a master demon hunter."

"Demon hunter, eh?" Steve asked.

"Yes," Scotty said. "I hunt other creatures as well. Demons are just where my specialty lies."

"Yo, Mick," Steve said. "You better watch out."

Scotty narrowed his eyes. "And why is that?"

Steve grabbed Mick's shoulder and laughed. "Because my boy here is a beast of the night."

"Excuse me?" Scotty asked.

"A werewolf," Mick cut-in. "But it's totally under control. I'm not, like, dangerous or nothing."

There was a long bout of silence as Scotty blinked incessantly. I glanced at Andy and raised my eyebrow. She returned my look with a shrug. After what felt like forever, Scotty shot to his feet and booked it to the room at the back of his trailer.

"Uh… dude?" Steve called after him.

No response.

"Is he okay?" Andy asked.

"Not sure," I said.

We could hear Scotty tossing things around the room and slamming drawers. Something just didn't feel right, so I got to my feet and headed for the back.

"You guys wait here," I said.

"Good luck," Mick mumbled.

"Yeah," Steve added, "Dude's totally lost his marbles."

I approached the door to the back room and gently pushed it open. The room was covered in wood paneling and had a single, un-made bed tucked in the corner. Scotty sat on it with his back facing me as he fiddled with a metal lock box. When he finally pried it open, he pulled out a steel revolver with a long, thin barrel. My heart leapt from my chest, and I rushed into the room.

"What the hell is that?" I asked.

"A revolver," he said casually as he fiddled with a box of bullets. "I know you're new to this whole Venator thing, but it's pretty basic. You see a creature, you hunt it."

"*Hunt* it?

"Yes."

"You don't mean…"

"I have two words for you, Charlie." He snapped the chamber shut and spun it. "Silver. Bullet."

As he got to his feet, I slammed the door shut and pressed my back against it.

"Move aside," he said.

"No."

He clenched his jaw. "Move. Aside."

"No," I said again.

We stared each other down until it was clear I wasn't going to budge. He cursed at me and dug his elbow into my side in an attempt to move me. I shoved him right back. Before I knew it, we were on the floor and I was able to pry the gun from his hands and slide it across the floor. He dove after it, but I wrapped my arms around him and pinned on his stomach. At the same time, the door burst open and my friends came barreling into the room.

"Grab the gun," I managed to grunt out as I struggled to keep Scotty still. "Hurry, he's trying to shoot Mick."

Mick's jaw dropped. "He's *what*?"

Andy quickly grabbed the gun and cradled it as if it were coated in poison.

"Get back, you beast!" Scotty shouted as he squirmed beneath me. He must've realized he wasn't going anywhere because he finally went limp. "Dammit, Charlie, you're supposed to hunt creatures, not befriend them! You have to be the worst Venator I've ever met."

"Wait," Mick said. "You were for real gonna shoot me?"

"I still plan to," Scotty snarled.

"Yo, that's messed up," Steve said.

With one final push, I finally got Scotty's hand's secured behind his back. As he laid beneath me, I thought about that black belt in Shotokan that he'd mentioned and wondered just how truthful he'd been.

"No one is getting shot," I said. "Yeah, Mick's a werewolf, but you heard him, it's under control."

"That doesn't matter," Scotty said. "As long as he lives, there's a chance he can pass on his genetics. He might not be dangerous, but who's to say his children or his children's children won't be?"

"Okay," I said. "But you can't just go around shooting people."

"Yeah," Steve added. "This ain't *Old* fuckin' *Yeller*."

"I will do what's necessary," Scotty said. "I might not be a Venator, but I still took the oath."

"The oath?" I asked.

"Yes," he said. "To rid the world of the purest of evils. It might not always be the easiest thing to do, but it's what I swore my life to do. Just leave me alone in a room with that stupid mutt, and I swear, I'll—"

I dug my knee harder into his back until he groaned.

"Christ, fine!" he shouted. "I won't hurt your pet dog. But from here on out, if we come across any other creatures, I will not be so kind. Got it?"

I glanced at my friends, and they nodded in approval, so I climbed from his back and we both stood. I eyed him and held my breath, afraid he might try something. He dusted off his pants and looked me up and down with his lips pursed. After a moment, he turned on his heel and marched back to the kitchen in a huff. I looked at my friends and shrugged before following after him.

There was a heavy silence as we sat around the kitchen table. It was sort of hard to move past the fact that Scotty had just tried to execute Mick. It was also hard not to crack a smile at Scotty's disheveled hair or the way his red bandana hung crooked on his forehead. Steve was the first to let out a stifled laugh.

"Let's focus," Scotty said, adjusting his bandana. "The Dybbuk. Charlie, I am going to need you to really dig down and think. What else can you tell me about them? We have a lack of leads, so even the smallest detail can help."

I forced my grin away and nodded, though there really wasn't all that much to add. I mean, I didn't even know what a Dybbuk was until that afternoon. It was then my mind flashed to Edgar. It wasn't much, but it was something.

"My neighbor," I said. "The other night. I saw him through his window. He was making these creepy wicker dolls."

Scotty's eyebrows shot up. "And you didn't think to tell me this before?"

"Sorry," I said.

"I don't get it," Steve cut in. "So, he was making wicker dolls. Who gives a crap?"

"I do," Scotty said, his tone sharp. "Wicker is a highly magical substance used for black magic."

The corner of Steve's lips tugged to a grin. "For real? *Wicker*? Shit, my Nana uses that stuff to make baskets during craft time at her retirement home. You think she's dabbling in the dark arts?"

Scotty rolled his eyes and turned back to me. "What can you tell me about your neighbor?"

"Not much," I said.

"Well, what's his name?" he asked.

"Edgar," I answered. "I only talked to him once. He was pretty nice actually. He's also got these weird burn scars all over his face."

"Do you know how he got them?" he asked.

"No idea," I said.

He stroked his chin. "Well, since this is our only lead, I suggest we poke around his place to see what we can find. At the very least, we can steal one of those wicker dolls and figure out what he's doing with them. How does that sound?"

We all agreed and began to set up a plan to meet in the parking lot after school the next day. From there, we'd spend the evening staking out Edgar's place. It wasn't much, but Scotty was right, it was our only lead.

As we left his trailer that evening, I felt a bit better knowing that we at least had a plan.

I just hoped Scotty knew what he was doing.

Edgar's house was just about as boring as you could possibly get. It was small and gray and had no garden or any sort of decor aside from an old, rusting ladder that'd been left unused and propped against the garage for weeks. His mailbox was plain and black, his front curtains were drawn shut, and he had a single, lonely sedan parked in his driveway. In the backyard was a monster sized bay window surrounded by trees and bushes. That evening, my friends and I ducked behind a particularly large evergreen shrub and took turns using Scotty's binoculars to watch Edgar through the window.

We had met earlier that day in the parking lot after school. It wasn't hard at all to find Scotty's truck as it was the only one with a big wooden crucifix hanging from the rearview mirror and spikes poking out from his hubcaps. We found him leaning against his bumper, decked out in camouflage and war paint. My friends wore their typical black garb, aside from Steve who opted to wear a bright purple *Cramps* t-shirt. Scotty immediately threw a fit and started ranting about the proper attire for a steak out. He was just about to start in on Andy with her bright blue hair, but I was able to calm him down. It wasn't until the sun started to go down that we finally made it to Edgar's place.

Edgar got home around six that evening with a bag of groceries in hand and for an hour straight, we watched him cook. Just cook. Nothing more. First, he fixed himself a glass of whiskey then proceeded to wash the vegetables and peel the potatoes. There was a tiny spike in excitement when he brought out a large collection of sharp butcher knives, but that quickly died down as soon as he used them to slice up a slab of meat.

"He's still cooking," Andy said as she peered through the binoculars. "The guy's got all four stove burners going and just put something in the oven. I don't think he's stopping anytime soon."

"Is he at least cooking up human flesh?" Steve asked.

"Just veggies," she said.

"Lame," he responded. "Aside from those gnarly burn scars, the dude's a total yawn-fest."

Scotty snatched the binoculars from Andy and placed them to his eyes.

"Patience," he said. "This is a stake out, not a rock and roll concert. Besides, this is only phase one." He nodded across the yard to a pair of old, wooden cellar doors. "I noticed he has a separate entrance to his basement. Once the opportunity presents itself, I plan to break in and investigate."

"How?" Andy asked. "Those doors are chained shut."

"I brought bolt cutters," he said.

"You serious?" she asked.

"Yes," he said.

"You know that's breaking and entering, right?" she asked.

"I'm aware," he said. "What did you think we came here to do, watch him cook a filet mignon? A thorough investigation always involves a bit of rule breaking. I know it's risky, but it'll be worth it in the end."

"Yo, you can count me in," Steve said. "I can't stand watching *Chef Boyardee* for another minute."

"Same here," Mick said.

Scotty scrunched his nose in disgust. "You see? Even the mutt gets it."

Mick rolled his eyes. "Oh, screw you."

Scotty ignored him and turned to me. "What do you say, Charlie?"

I glanced at Andy and raised my eyebrows. I'd never really been one to break the law, but if ever there was a time to do so, I figured this was it. I eventually pushed my hair from my face and shrugged.

"I guess I'm in," I said.

She pursed her lips a moment before letting out a breath. "Whatever. Let's just get this over with."

"Wonderful," Scotty said.

We went back to watching Edgar cook. It felt like an eternity before he finally started to clean the dishes and separate the meal into several plastic containers. I found it odd that he spent all that time cooking and never took a single bite, but that thought fell to the back of my mind once he flicked off the lights and made his way upstairs.

Wasting no time, Scotty darted from behind the bushes and we followed after him. My pulse picked up in speed until we stopped at the cellar doors. They were positioned right below the window, so we had to crouch down in order to not be seen. I noticed the wood of the doors was older and rotting in a few places while the chain and lock holding them together was brand new and scuff free. As soon as Scotty pulled out his pair of bolt cutters, my eyes went wide. He didn't even give us a warning before he cut the chain with a loud crack. I held my breath and waited for footsteps or a light to flick on, but thankfully, there was nothing.

"All right, shut up and listen," Scotty whispered. "I think two of us should go down to explore while the rest keep lookout. Since I'm the most qualified, I'll go down. Who's going with me?"

"I'll do it," I said.

"No way," Mick cut in. "He knows where you live. I'll go."

"I'm the smallest," Andy said. "You don't know what's down

there. I might have to fit in tight spaces.”

“Shit,” Steve said. “Now I gotta volunteer or else I look like an asshole.”

“It has to be me,” I said. “I’m the Venator.”

“No,” Mick said. “That doesn’t—”

“For the love of god,” Scotty grumbled. “I’m touched you’re all willing to put yourselves on the line, but we don’t have time for this crap. Charlie’s right; it has to be him. Aside from me, he knows the most about the supernatural world. He might be able to spot things you guys wouldn’t.”

Mick glanced at Andy with his brow furrowed before letting out a breath. “I guess you got a point.”

“Yeah,” Andy said. “But just be careful, all right?”

“Of course,” I replied.

“Super,” Scotty said, his tone flat. “Now let’s get a move on.”

He started down the staircase, and I gave my friends one last look before taking the plunge after him. The stairs were steep and made of rickety old wood that seemed to creek with each step I took. When I got to the bottom, I inhaled a thick cloud of dust and had to bury my face in my sleeve to keep from coughing.

“Here,” Scotty said, handing me a flashlight. “Let’s split up. Well cover more ground that way.”

“Got it,” I said.

I forced one foot in front of the other and began my descent into the darkness. From what I could tell, the basement was way bigger than I’d previously thought and seemed to have no end in sight. It reminded me of a dungeon with its gravel floors and cement walls. I could even see little dust particles floating through the beam of light from my flashlight. I had to move slow and make sure with every step that I didn't trip in a ditch or run into one of the many low hanging beams.

I got started right away and began digging through a stack of boxes. At first, it was kind of exciting as I had no idea what sort of weird crap I'd find, but that energy quickly died down when the only thing I found was a stack of cracked dishware and some random tools. I pushed them aside and opened another box, but time after time it was the same deal—a bunch of useless junk. I figured maybe he kept the good stuff buried closer to the back, so I got to my feet and trekked on. Unfortunately, all I found was a broken set of patio furniture and some old VHS tapes. In fact, the further I delved into the depths of the basement, the more I lost hope. I'd been poking around for close to half an hour when I finally stumbled across a staircase that was different than the one I'd come down. I figured it led to Edgar's house and realized then that I must've finally reached the opposite wall. It was official; there was nothing. Absolutely nothing. I sighed in defeat and hoped Scotty had more luck than I did.

Just as I was about to turn around and head back, my flashlight shined over a bookcase. It was made of mahogany wood and packed to the brim with books, but the thing that stood out the most was how clean it was compared to everything else; it was clear someone used it often. Curious, I shuffled over and pulled out the first book I could get my hands on. The cover was leather-bound with a gold engraving that read *The Master of Ballantrae* by Robert Louis Stevenson. I'd never heard of it before, but a quick skim through the pages told me it was a fiction novel that had to have dated back to the eighteen hundreds. It was cool, but not exactly the sort of thing I was looking for, so I placed it back on the shelf and pulled out another. Same deal—a classic fiction novel that was as old as sin, but at least I'd heard of this one before. *Catch-22* by Joseph Heller; my dad had a copy he kept in our trailer. I placed it back and pulled out a few more duds before I finally came across one that caused me to pause.

It was a red book with no title but rather a simple picture on the cover of a dagger pierced through the head of a wolf. I stared at it with my brow scrunched. That image. I'd seen it before. In fact, I'd seen it many times; it resembled the tattoo across my father's chest. I pried it open, and the spine cracked. One look at the dust-ridden pages told me that this book was long forgotten. I was hardly able to shine my light over the first page when I heard a loud *creek* from above.

I jumped back, nearly dropping the book. The sound continued to grow louder by the second. My pulse raced when I realized what it was. Footsteps. They were moving fast—someone was coming. Far across the basement, I noticed Scotty making his way up the cellar stairs. He was safe. *Safe*. God, I wished I was with him, but he was so far, and there was way too much junk blocking my path; I'd never make it. Just then, the basement door swung open, and my blood turned to ice. Without thinking, I tucked the book under my arm and dove behind an antique armoire.

The footsteps continued down the stairs, one after the other. I shuddered when they finally reached the bottom and a single weak light bulb flicked on. The room filled with silence as I pressed my back hard against the armoire. I waited anxiously for Edgar to move or speak or at least do something because the lack of sound was killing me. But when he finally moved, it sent my heart into spasms. Closer and closer he drew toward me. I closed my eyes, not daring to take a single breath until he stopped at the bookcase next to me. I bit down hard on my lip in attempts to stifle my heavy breathing. I couldn't see him, but I could hear him thumbing through his book collection. He pulled one out and turned the page which seemed to echo around the entire basement like thunder. And then he began to whistle. It was a sharp, aggressive sound that stabbed at my ear drums that I finally recognized to be *Mr. Sandman* by the Chordettes.

By this point, I was sweating through my shirt. All the while, Edgar just kept whistling and turning pages. He'd grab a new book. Whistling. Turning pages. *Mr. Sandman, bring me a dream. Make him the cutest that I've ever seen. Give him two lips, like roses and clover, and tell him that his lonesome nights are over.* I was so caught up in the tune that I nearly jumped out of my skin when the doorbell rang.

I immediately gasped and slapped my hands over my mouth. At the same time, his whistling ceased. Silence. I dug my fingers into my face until I felt pain, hoping like hell he didn't hear me. For the longest time, there was nothing. No movement. No sound. I just waited. Time stood still until finally, he turned on his heel and headed up the stairs. I let out a sigh of relief, and the second the door closed behind him, I sprinted for the exit. I definitely made more noise than I probably should've, but I couldn't help myself.

When I finally made it outside, I placed my hands behind my head and took a long breath. God, the air never tasted so sweet. I inhaled deeply, savoring every precious breath, when Scotty appeared at my side.

"Good to see you've made it," he said.

"The doorbell," I said, my chest still tight. "Someone rang it. I was able to sneak out."

"Yes, I know."

"You do?"

"Of course, considering I was the one who rang it." He glanced over his shoulder before grabbing me and pulling me along. "Come on, let's get out of here. I told the others to meet at my truck."

We crouched low and cut through the yard. When I climbed into the passenger's seat of Scotty's truck, I was surprised to find my friends already piled in back. As soon as I closed the door behind me, Mick leaned across the center console, grabbed my face with both hands, and kissed me hard on the cheek.

"Thank fucking Christ you're alive," he said.

"Yeah," Andy added. "We thought you were a goner. You okay?"

"I'm fine," I said.

Steve punched my shoulder. "Well, that's a damn relief. It woulda been a total bummer if that Edgar guy sliced and diced you into a million little pieces and threw you in his salad, dude."

I forced a smile. "Thanks Steve."

Scotty climbed in through the driver's side door and waved his hand. "Yes, yes, we're all so very glad Charlie's not dead, but let's focus on what's important." He snatched the book from my lap. "I saw you carrying this. Great find!"

"What is it?" I asked.

He frowned. "You mean you don't know?"

"Not exactly," I said.

"Then why'd you grab it?" he asked.

I shrugged. "My dad had this picture tattooed on his chest. Figured it might be important."

"Well, you figured right," he said. "This right here is the single most sacred symbol in the history of Venator. It's called *The Founder's Wolf*. And I'm not surprised your dad had it tattooed on his chest. It's tradition for Venators to get this image marked on their bodies once they complete training. In fact…" He began tugging at his shirt sleeve and rolled it past his wrist to reveal a tattoo similar to my father's. "I got this when I was thirteen."

"Whoa," Steve said. "Sick ink, dude."

"Does this mean Edgar's a Venator?" Andy asked.

"Maybe," he said. "Maybe not. We honestly can't know for sure, but at least this is a start." He glanced at his watch. "Anyway, I think we should wrap up for the night. Let's reconvene tomorrow morning before school to come up with our next plan of action. Good work everyone."

After we said our goodbyes, I hopped out of the truck. The second they drove off, I stole a quick glance at Edgar's place and a shiver crawled down my spine. There was just something about it. I couldn't quite put my finger on it, but the fact that it was so damn ordinary made it even worse. It was like there was a horrible monster hiding in plain sight. Not only that, *in my backyard.* I shook it off and headed inside because truth be told, I was totally exhausted and couldn't wait to pass out.

I walked through the front door to find Aunt Joy sitting on the living room couch. She was fiddling with a spool of yarn and watching an episode of *The Golden Girls.* Her hair was wrapped in curlers and she had on her cheetah print house robe that usually meant she was in for the night. I kicked off my shoes as quietly as I could and started for the stairs, but before I could even take a step, she perked up.

"Oh Charlie, you're home," she said. "Good, I need help winding this yarn. Do you have a minute?"

I hesitated a moment and glanced at the stairs. Sleep sure sounded great, but my weakness was that I could never say no to her, so I nodded and made my way over to the couch. As soon as I sat, she positioned my hands in front of my face and began to wrap a bright pink ball of yarn around them.

"So, I saw you outside," she said.

My heart leapt from my chest. "You what?"

"I saw you outside," she said again.

"Oh, I-I wasn't—"

"Were those your friends?" she asked.

"Huh?"

"Out in the driveway." Her lip curled. "I'm sorry, honey. I didn't mean to spy on you. I just happened to notice the headlights in the driveway, so I peeked through the blinds and there you were. You know, you should've invited them inside for a bite to eat. I've been dying to meet them."

"Oh…"

I let out a sigh of relief when I realized she hadn't caught me snooping in the neighbor's yard.

"Maybe next time," I said.

"Is that a promise?"

"Yep."

She paused briefly before lowering the yarn. "Is everything all right, dear? You look like you just saw a ghost."

"I'm fine," I said quickly. "Just tired."

"You sure?"

I nodded.

As she looked me over, I forced a smile until she finally nodded and went back to winding the yarn. At the same time, my face fell; I hated lying to her, but I didn't know what else to do. It wasn't like I could just tell her that I was under a lot of pressure because our neighbor might be some psycho killer. I mean, I wanted to. Of course I did. God, I wanted to tell her *everything*, but I couldn't turn her life upside down like that. What kind of asshole would do something like that?

Just as my mind began that oh, so familiar dive down the rabbit hole of self-loathing, the doorbell rang. I perked up as Aunt Joy set down her ball of yarn and got to her feet. A strange feeling brewed in the pit of my stomach and continued to get worse until she finally opened the front door.

Edgar.

Suddenly, the walls closed in on me. There he was. Right there. Standing in our goddamn doorway. He had on a simple green vest and blue jeans as well as a plaid scarf that covered up much of the scarring on his neck. In his hands was one of the Tupperware containers from the meal he'd made earlier.

"Oh, Edgar," Aunt Joy said. "What a nice surprise. How're you?"

"I'm doing wonderful," he said. "I apologize for the late night visit, but I was hoping you could help me with something." He held out the food and smiled. "You see; it seems I've cooked this lovely meal only to realize I have no one to share it with. It's a thick cut sliced steak with porcini sauce and boursin creamed spinach; my specialty. Would you care to take it off my hands?"

Her face lit up as she took the food. "Wow, thank you! That's so kind of you. You know, Charlie and I were just sitting around watching television. Would you care to come in and join us?"

I snapped back to reality. Edgar. He was invited into our house. A rush of adrenaline shot through me, and I jumped to my feet.

"No!" I shouted.

Aunt Joy whipped around, her eyes wide with alarm. "Excuse me?"

Right away, the embarrassment burned through me. I began fidgeting with my sleeves, unable to look at either of them. "I just.… It's late. I have a test tomorrow. I need to get some sleep."

"Okay?" she said, her eyebrow raised. "Then just me and Edgar will hang out."

"No," I said again.

"Charlie," she snapped. "Why are you being so rude?"

"It's okay," Edgar cut in.

"No, it isn't," Aunt Joy said. "I'm so sorry, he's not normally like this."

"Don't worry about it," Edgar said. "Besides, Charlie is right, it's getting late. I should get going."

"Are you sure?" she asked.

"Positive," he said. "You two have a nice night, and enjoy the steak. It pairs well with a Cabernet."

She smiled once more. "Thanks again, Edgar."

I sighed in relief as he turned to walk away, but then he stopped and my heart was right back in my throat.

"Oh, and one last thing," he said. "Earlier tonight, it appears as though someone had broken into my basement. Nothing was stolen, though I did want to warn you to keep an eye out for trespassers." His eyes flicked to mine. "There's a lot of bad people out there, Joy. You just can't trust anyone these days."

It was a punch to the gut. That look in his eye. It was just a quick glance, but it was packed with pure malice. He *knew* it was me. I watched in stunned silence as Aunt Joy thanked him and said goodbye, though I could hardly hear a single word; the blood pounding in my ears was deafening. It wasn't until she closed the door and turned to me with a scowl that I came back to.

"What on earth was that about?" she asked.

"I don't trust him," I said. "And I don't want him coming around the house when I'm not here."

"Oh, is that so?"

"Yes. He's bad news."

"*Edgar?*" She laughed and shook her head. "Don't be ridiculous, Charlie. I know he might look intimidating, but you can't judge a book by its cover. I mean, look at *me* for heaven's sake."

"It's… it's not that."

"Then what is it?"

I looked to my feet and shook my head. The truth was, I had no visible reason to hate Edgar; at least not a reason I could share with Aunt Joy. Her eyes were locked on me, waiting for an answer.

"That's what I thought," she said. "Edgar is a good man. Not to mention, an excellent cook. I mean, can you smell this steak?" She took the lid off the food container and pulled out a piece of steak. "Gosh, this just looks so delicious."

Panic shot through me and before I knew it, I rushed over and slapped the meat from her hand. Not only that, I knocked the entire Tupperware container to the floor, sending the steak and porcini sauce—or whatever the hell it was called—to splatter everywhere.

"Charlie!" she shrieked.

"I'm sorry," I said. "I had to. I think he might've poisoned it or something, I don't know!"

"*Poison?*" she said. "Have you lost your damn mind?"

"Maybe," I mumbled.

I recoiled into myself as she death glared me. I'd never seen her so mad; it was absolutely terrifying. But instead of blowing up further, her expression softened.

"Oh," she said. "I think I know what this is about."

"You do?" I asked.

"Its about your father, isn't it?"

My jaw dropped.

"Yes, of course," she went on, completely ignoring my totally confused expression. "This makes so much sense. How could I not have seen it before?"

I was completely dumbfounded as she grabbed my shoulder and led me to the couch to sit.

"Let me guess," she said. "When you see Edgar, you think of your father, don't you?"

"Huh? No, I—"

"Oh, Charlie. I'm so sorry."

"No, really. I—"

"It's okay," she said. "I understand your father hurt you, but that's no reason to assume all men are dangerous. Edgar did nothing wrong, honey. He's not the one you're angry with." She paused a moment and began stroking my hand. "You know, I've been thinking a lot lately, and I believe it'd be a good idea for you to start therapy. Especially after all you've been through. How does that sound?"

I blinked a few times, stunned into silence. I mean, this was probably the first time in my life where my father was not the root of my problems. And I most certainly did not want to do therapy. But I thought about it a bit more and realized if this got her to stay away from Edgar, then I'd play along, so I grit my teeth and nodded.

She kissed the top of my head. "Good. I love you, Charlie."

I love you, Charlie.

Edgar was suddenly pushed from my mind. Those damn words again. Before I could really process them, she was up the stairs.

She loved me.

She *loved* me.

And all I could do was sit there like a total doofus. God, what the hell was wrong with me?

I rubbed my hands over my face as my mind drifted back to Edgar. Focus. That creepy feeling in the pit of my stomach returned as I peeked out the window at his house and imagined him waiting for us to go to sleep so he could attack. I rushed to the door and quickly turned the lock.

Edgar was right.

You just can't trust anyone these days.

That night, I grabbed a blanket and pillow from my room and made myself a bed on the downstairs couch. I also slept with a baseball bat by my side; I didn't want Edgar to catch me off guard if for some reason he decided to murder my aunt and I in the middle of the night. I thought maybe the bat would give me some peace of mind, but it didn't. In fact, for the next few hours I tossed and turned like crazy.

I thought a lot about Edgar which was no surprise. But I also couldn't help but think about what Aunt Joy had said about my father. Maybe she was right. Maybe part of me was afraid of Edgar because he was a man. God, I hated the possibility that my father might've had even a slight lasting negative impact on my life. And the more I thought about it, the angrier I got, until I realized I'd been scratching at the scar on my stomach. The skin around it was a bright shade of red, and there were little specks of blood. I cursed and tugged my shirt down.

That night flashed to the forefront of my mind, and I gripped the bat so hard, my fists shook.

Calm down.

I took a deep breath and racked my brain for something to help ease my anger. I snatched the remote and turned on the television. The bright light filled the room as it flicked on to one of those insane, late night bible thumper shows. Reverend Donovan. He wore a cheap brown suit and had an obvious comb over. *And for just a small monthly donation of $19.99, your soul could be saved from eternal damnation!*

Right.

His voice was like nails on a chalkboard, but at least it was a distraction. I listened to him for a while, completely fascinated by how red and blotchy his face got as he ranted about the plagues of Egypt. The livestock and the locusts. The blood on the doors. Something about a sacrificial lamb. It was kind of soothing in a weird way. For the longest time, I just stared at the television like a total zombie. That is, until he said something that caused me to snap out of my daze and perk up. *Moses stretched out his hand toward the sky, and total darkness covered all Egypt for three days. No one could see anyone else or leave his place for three days.*

I blinked a few times. The longer the words bounced around my head, the faster my heart began to race.

Darkness.

Total darkness.

It was then that it fully clicked in my brain, and I sat up. I could hear Andy's voice as clear as day.

The four horsemen of the apocalypse.

It was like a freight train crashed into me. Scotty. He'd been ranting about Midtowne and the darkness ever since the fire. And the disease that's been killing all the local crops. It was just like the locusts that plagued Egypt. Darkness. Disease. War. Virtue. I remember reading that in order to call upon the Four Horsemen, you had to break each seal one at a time. The thought was enough to send my stomach to my knees.

Not wanting to waste another second, I rushed to the front window and peered at Edgar's darkened house. My body was running on pure adrenaline. Could he really be trying to summon the horsemen? And if he was, *why*? I thought about that bookcase in his basement. He could've had a book just like my father's. An instruction manual on how to break the seals. Before I knew it, I had grabbed a flashlight from a kitchen drawer and was out the front door. It was a fire that burned inside me and demanded answers. I just had to get back in Edgar's basement and search his bookcase once more. God, it could've been staring at my right in the damn face; if only I'd seen it.

It wasn't until I was creeping behind the bushes in front of his house that I truly realized what I was doing. I was breaking into Edgar's basement. This time alone. No one to ring the doorbell. No one to hear my screams. It'd all happened so damn fast. The adrenaline slowed as I approached his cellar doors, but I had gone too far to turn back at that point. I took a deep breath and turned on my flashlight. That's when I heard a voice from behind that caused my hair to stand on end.

I whipped around so fast, I dropped the flashlight. In the dim moonlight, I could see Edgar's silhouette. It was too dark to catch a good read on his expression, but based on his tone of voice, it was clear he wasn't exactly thrilled to see me. I was overwhelmed with panic and began looking around for a way to escape.

"It'd be in your best interest not to run," he said as if reading my mind.

"I-I wasn't—"

"There's no need to lie, Charlie." He placed his arm around me. "Come now, let's have a little chat."

His long, spindly fingers gripped my shoulder like a tarantula wrapping around its prey. This was it. Death. And I just followed along like a helpless lamb ready for slaughter. My heart thumped as he led me through the back door and into his kitchen—that same kitchen where I had watched him slice and dice his dinner with his vast collection of sharp knives. I swallowed and looked around, surprised at how immaculate it was. The floor was scrubbed to perfection, his walls a stark white. I couldn't help but wonder how long it'd take him to wash the blood away. And no doubt he'd be able to eliminate any trace I was ever there.

He sat me down at the kitchen table. My brain screamed at my legs to run, but I was too paralyzed with fear. I looked around for ways to escape, when he slipped a glass of water in front of me.

"Drink up," he said. "You seem a bit nervous."

"I-I…." I paused and gained control of my shaking voice. "I'm not thirsty."

"No?"

I shook my head.

He nodded and took the seat next to me, though his eyes never left mine. He crossed his legs and folded his hands on the table in one swift move before looking to me with a knowing smirk.

"I know it was you sneaking around my basement earlier," he said. "Tell me, what exactly was it you were looking for?"

I remained silent; my only defense.

The tension in the room grew uncomfortable to the point where I thought I was going to snap, but then he shook his head and let out the creepiest damn laugh I'd ever heard.

"Bravo, Charlie," he said. "You've figured out that I'm a Venator. That much is obvious considering you stole my book."

He tugged up his sleeve to reveal the Founder's Wolf, only his tattoo was a bit different from Scotty's. Instead of ink, a brand had seared his skin. He looked to the mark with malice in his eyes before his eyes flicked up to meet mine.

"I know what you are," he said, his voice slow and calculated.

"I'm not—"

"Don't lie to me," he snapped. "I could tell just by looking at you.

Venators are all the same. Let me guess, your father started training when you were a young boy. Five, maybe six years old, perhaps? I'm sure he hammered into your head all those arbitrary rules before teaching you to hunt. And now here you are, a good little soldier just like your father. Yes, I bet you're just like him."

"That's not true," I said, surprising even myself with how sharp my tone was.

"Excuse me?"

"I'm nothing like him," I said. "I'll *never* be like him."

It was then that I realized I'd been clenching my fists so tight, they shook. I released my grip and took a few breaths. When I finally calmed, I noticed Edgar staring at me, only this time, it was as if all the anger had left him and he was a new person. His eyes studied every last inch of me as if he could see through to my soul. I looked to my lap and began fiddling with the ends of my sleeve.

"Sorry," I said, finally breaking the unbearable silence. "It's just... I didn't exactly get along with my father."

"No?"

I shook my head.

His gaze still seared into me.

"The scar on your face," he said finally. "Your father. He did that to you. That's why you live with your aunt. And your mother died in childbirth, didn't she?"

"H-how'd you know all that?" I asked.

"So it's true?"

I nodded, but I didn't dare look at him. My stomach twisted in knots as the silence grew thick. Finally, he reached across the table but along the way, he bumped into my water glass. It knocked over, causing water to spill everywhere.

He cursed and shot to his feet. "I'm such an idiot."

"It's okay," I said.

"No, it isn't. Here, let me clean this up for you."

He darted to the kitchen and began opening and closing every last drawer until he finally found a roll of paper towels. I watched with my brow raised as he wiped the spill. His hands were shaking and his face was pale; something just didn't seem right. When he was finally done, he sat back down and covered his mouth with his hand.

"I'm sorry," he said. "I just wasn't expecting this."

"Expecting what?"

"That you…." He placed both hands on the table and inhaled deeply. "Charlie, there's something you need to know about. Many years ago, there was a curse placed upon the Venators by a coven of witches in an attempt to end the Venator bloodline. It made it so that any woman carrying a Venator's blood in her womb was destined to die in childbirth. The father would be left with a violent rage, one that would inevitably overpower him and drive him to murder the child. I was warned of it my entire life, but I never truly believed it until now." He placed his hands on the table and looked at me dead in the eye. "Charlie, just like you, I had a mother who died in childbirth. And just like you, I grew up with a wretched man for a father. It was no coincidence. It was because of this curse."

I stared at the table, too dazed to move let alone speak. Finally, Edgar placed his hand on mine.

"You can talk to me," he said.

"It's just…" I closed my eyes as a lump grew in my throat. "I don't really know what to say."

"You don't have to say anything," he said. "I know exactly what you're feeling. My father tried to take my life as well. It was two weeks before my eighteenth birthday. I awoke to the smell of gasoline. And then I realized my clothes and hair were damp. Before I could put it all together, my father lit the match. I wake up every single morning in a panic for fear that he's standing over me. Every single morning, Charlie. While it might've been the curse that drove him to insanity, it was still him that lit the match."

The room fell silent. I watched as he clenched and unclenched his fists. That anger he felt. I knew it all too well. For the first time in my life, it felt as though someone finally understood.

"My father," I said softly. "He was drunk. Whiskey; I'll never forget the smell. He used broken glass to stab me and then slit his wrists. If it wasn't for the neighbors, we'd both be dead."

"He's still alive?"

"Yeah," I said. "He's in some mental hospital just outside of Richmond."

I closed my eyes and waited for a panic attack to start. I waited for my nerves to overwhelm me. For the sweat. The shaking hands. But nothing happened. For the first time, I felt empowered.

"I'm so sorry that happened to you," Edgar said. "Do you feel as though you could forgive him someday?"

"No," I said quickly.

"Are you sure? Perhaps he—"

"No." I clenched my fists and looked him dead in the eye. "I will never forgive my father as long as I live. I don't give a crap if he was cursed or not. For eighteen years, I lived in hell. He did that. Not some curse."

He stared at me for the longest time, almost as if he was trying to get a read on me. Finally, the corner of his lip curled. "You have no idea how glad I am to hear you say that, Charlie."

I wasn't sure exactly what he meant by that, but before I could say anything else he cut in.

"May I ask you something?"

"Sure," I said.

"It's a bit of a change in subject, but I'm curious. Why were you snooping around my basement?"

"Oh, that," I said, my face turning red. "Well, uh… it's sort of hard to explain, but my friends and I all thought you might've been the one behind the fire back in September."

"Me?"

"Yeah, I know. It's dumb."

"What on earth made you think that?" he said with a chuckle.

"I don't know," I said. "I guess a while back I saw you making these wicker dolls. My friend got me all paranoid and said wicker was used for black magic and it sort of spiraled from there." Just then it hit me and I scrunched my brow. "Hang on, why *were* you making those dolls?"

He grinned. "Your friend was quite right, Charlie. Wicker is in fact used for black magic, but only when it's in the wrong hands. I can assure you, I was only using it for research purposes. With all that's been going on around town with the fire and then the suicides, I have reason to believe those things are tied together. And considering that I found wicker at the scene of the crime, I decided to do a bit of research."

I suddenly remembered just why I had been snooping at Edgar's house that night. The book. The four horsemen. It all came flooding back.

"The book," I whispered.

"Excuse me?"

"Sorry," I said. "It's just…. I need to talk to you about something. It's this book my father had when I was a kid. It had to do with the four horsemen of the apocalypse. I think someone is trying to summon them. It'd explain why Midtowne's been all dark ever since the fire and the crops dying and I don't know. I haven't really put much thought into it yet. But do you think that's crazy?"

"Not at all," he said. "I think you're really onto something."

"You do?"

"Absolutely," he said. "In fact, I'd love it if you'd come by my place more often to discuss these theories you have. Perhaps we could work together." He paused a moment before adding, "And that friend you mentioned earlier. The one who knew about the wicker."

"You mean Scotty?"

"Yes," he said. "I'd quite like to meet him. He sounds like he could be a valuable asset. Would you mind inviting him over as well?"

"Sure, I guess," I said.

"Wonderful." He checked his watch. "It's getting late. We should call it a night before your aunt wakes up to find you missing. Joy seems like a strong woman; I wouldn't want to get on her bad side."

We pushed out our chairs and got to our feet. Before I knew it, his hand was on my shoulder. This time, instead of feeling like a tarantula attacking me, it was more gentle, like a friend.

"I really enjoyed talking with you tonight," he said. "You and I, we have this connection. You remind me of me when I was your age."

"Really?"

"Yes, does that worry you?"

I smirked. "No, I guess not. You know, I'm really glad you caught me breaking into your basement tonight."

He gave my shoulder one last squeeze and grinned. "As am I,

Charlie."

We said our goodbyes and he walked me to the front door rather than the back. I went home that night feeling refreshed. For the first time in a long time, I felt hope. Me and Edgar. We were a team. And with his help, I was sure we'd be able to figure out what was going on around town and put a stop to it. In fact, the second I laid my head on my pillow, I was out like a light.

It was the best sleep I'd had in years.

The next morning, I met my friends under the bleachers at the school gymnasium. I told them all about Edgar and the complete one-eighty he pulled on me the night before. I also mentioned what he'd said about my father's book and how he thought it made sense. The only thing I left out was the curse. I wasn't quite ready to talk about that with my friends just yet. It felt too personal; like a secret between Edgar and me. When I was finally done talking, they stared at me in shock.

"So, let me get this straight," Steve said. "Jerry freakin' Dandridge is *not* the bad guy after all that?"

"Guess not," I said.

"Damn, what a waste of a perfectly good villain," he said. "He had that look down pat with all those burn scars."

"He could be lying," Andy suggested.

"No," Scotty chimed in. "I don't think he is. Last night, he was all alone with Charlie. No one knew he was over there. If he was going to pull something, that would've been the perfect time to do it, but he didn't." He turned to me. "That book you mentioned. The four horsemen. You mentioned it was your father's?"

"Yeah," I said.

"What else can you tell me about it?"

"Not much. I mean, I've already told you everything I know."

"Well, that's not good enough," he said, "I want to know that book inside and out. What the horsemen are capable of. How to summon them and how to stop them. We're going to have to talk with someone who can get me the answers I need."

"Edgar told me he doesn't know much either," I said.

"I'm not talking about Edgar."

"Then who…" My voice trailed off as it dawned on me just who he was talking about. In a split second, my palms began to sweat and my stomach twisted. "No. Absolutely not! No goddamn way!"

"What is it?" Mick asked.

"He wants to talk to my *father*!" I shouted.

"Oh, come on," Scotty said. "This book is a great lead. The problem is, we don't know enough about it. Your father does. If we are going to move forward on this, we need to talk to him."

"You don't understand," I said. "My father hates me. You think he's gonna help me?"

"It's worth a shot," Scotty said.

"No. It's not."

"Are you serious?"

"Dead serious. There's no way in hell I'm visiting him."

"You've got to be kidding me," he snapped. "The fate of the world is at stake. Are you really this selfish?"

"Yes," I said bluntly.

"Unbelievable." He threw his hands in the air and huffed. "I swear, Charlie, you're as stubborn as a damn mule."

"I could go with you," Andy piped up. "You know, as support. As much as I hate to admit it, he's right, Charlie. We're backed in a corner. Talking to your dad might at least point us in the right direction."

"Told you," Scotty mumbled.

I ignored him and looked to her, my heart pounding. She half smiled and grabbed my hand.

"It'll be okay," she said.

Her skin was soft and warm. It was comforting. After a moment, I pinched the bridge of my nose and let out a breath.

"Screw it," I said. "Fine."

"So we can go?" Scotty asked.

"Yeah, whatever," I mumbled.

Scotty pumped his fist into the air. "Thank Christ! So where can we find him?"

"He's at a hospital near Ladysmith," I said. "It's just over an hour away."

"Can we go tonight?" he asked.

"I'm pretty sure they only allow visitors on the weekend," I said.

"There's a full moon this weekend," Mick cut in. "I should probably stay back just to be safe."

"I'll hang with you," Steve suggested.

"Thank, man." Mick turned to me. "You guys can go on Saturday and swing by my place after?"

Scotty sneered. "Disgusting. You can count me out. I'd be too tempted to put a bullet through your heart."

Mick stuck up his middle finger. "As if you're invited, butthead."

Scotty slapped his hand away, and before it got any more heated, Andy stepped between them. When the tension finally eased, we all agreed to the plans before going our separate ways. I was pretty dazed at first, but the second I was alone, it really hit me. I was going to see my father. God, I was going to see my *father*. A wave of nausea hit me as I walked into homeroom. I thought I might pass out, but I pushed through it and found a seat near the back. I spent the rest of the day counting down the seconds until school was out. I just couldn't focus.

I hightailed it home, and for the rest of the afternoon, I was posted up in Aunt Joy's living room and basically stalked Edgar's place until I saw his car roll up the driveway. At that point, the sun was just dipping over the horizon and the street lights flickered on. I rushed over and rang the bell, waiting anxiously for him to answer; I just had to talk to someone that would understand. As soon as the door swung open, he lit up.

"Charlie," he said. "Good to see you."

"Is this a bad time?" I asked.

"No, no, not at all," he said. "In fact, I was hoping you'd stop by." He glanced over my shoulder. "Did you bring your friend?"

"No," I said.

He shrugged it off. "Oh, well, that's no worry. Please, come in."

I followed him to his living room, where much like his kitchen, it was pristine. He had a sleek white sofa and a clean beige carpet. Across from the couch was a stone fireplace and a wooden mantle that held several potted plants. As soon as we sat, a rush of nerves took over, and the words just sort of fell out.

"I'm gonna visit my father," I said.

"Excuse me?"

"This Sunday." I pressed my hand to my forehead and took a breath. "I told my friends about the book, and now they think it'd be a good idea to visit him and see if we can get any more information, but I don't know. I really don't wanna go. Like, not at all, but they don't get it."

He stared at me, his face void of any emotion. After a moment, he folded his hands on his lap and sighed.

"I hate to say it," he said. "But I agree with your friends."

"You *do*?"

"Yes," he said. "I know this is difficult, Charlie, but I really think we're on the right path with this book. Unfortunately, we've reached a dead end, but talking to you father could open new doors."

My body deflated as I looked to my lap.

Truth be told, I was really hoping Edgar would be on my side. The fact that he wasn't was a hard blow to take. He must've noticed my disappointment because he placed a hand on my shoulder.

"I understand you're nervous," he said. "You'll try to find every reason not to go, but trust me on this. It'll be worth it. And not just to find more information on that book. Think about it. This is your chance to tell your father what you really think of him. How much you *loathe* him. Your father has no power over you anymore, Charlie. You can finally stand up to him."

"I don't know if I can do that," I said.

"Why not?"

"Because I'm *me*." I pushed the hair from my face and shrugged. "The truth is, I'm a total wimp."

"You're not," he said. "Not at all. In fact, I was just like you when I was your age. Anxious. Insecure. But when I stood up to my father, it was the single greatest moment of my life. I was able to release *years* of pent up anger, and from that moment on, I felt a new strength. I'm a different man. I truly think you'd regret not doing this."

I dropped my chin to my chest. As much as I didn't want to admit it, Edgar was probably right. Standing up to my father could be a good thing, and deep down I knew I should take advantage of it.

"I guess you're right," I said.

"I know I am. Trust me, this will be good for you."

"I hope so."

"If it makes it any easier, you could stop by my place afterwards to tell me all about it. You could even bring your friends; I'd love to meet them."

"Sure," I said.

"Fantastic. I'm really looking forward to this, Charlie. I know you're not going to regret it."

The plan was set, and oddly enough, as I walked home I wasn't as nervous as I thought I'd be. Edgar's very presence calmed me. He made me feel like things were going to be all right. I was not used to having someone I could open up to, and I mean *truly* open up. I loved Aunt Joy to death, but I couldn't even begin to imagine talking to her about this sort of thing. By the time I left that evening, I felt confident even though I still couldn't even fully process that I was going to see my father on Sunday. I was going to see him, but not only that, I was going to stand up to him.

Edgar was right; I could do this.

That night, I spent a good amount of time staring at the ceiling in a vacant daze. It must've been seven in the morning when I finally decided to just give up on sleep altogether. I rolled out of bed and threw on a pair of jeans before heading downstairs. I was surprised to find Aunt Joy standing over the stove, frying up a pan of eggs.

"Oh, Charlie," she said, glancing over her shoulder. "You're up early."

"I couldn't sleep," I said, rubbing my face.

"Everything okay?"

I nodded.

She narrowed her eyes and looked me over. I was sure I looked like total crap and waited for her to tell me as much, but after a moment, she just shrugged it off.

"Why don't you take a seat?" she asked. "I don't have to work today, so I figured I'd cook us some breakfast."

I wasn't sure what else to do, so I plopped down at the kitchen table. There was a small, portable radio next to her, and she hummed and bobbed her hips along to the soft sounds of Lou Reed. When she was finally done, she placed two steaming plates of eggs and bacon on the table and sat next to me. As she happily chomped away, I stared at my food and fought the urge to hurl. She must've noticed my unease because after a while, she placed her fork and knife down and sighed.

"All right," she said. "Out with it."

"What?"

"Give it a rest. I think I know you well enough now to realize when something's bothering you."

I shifted in my seat.

"Oh, Charlie," she said. "You know you can talk to me about anything, right? Anything at all."

"Yeah, I know," I said softly.

"Well, then…" She picked up her fork and knife and began picking at her eggs. "I hope that whatever's on your mind, you feel comfortable enough to come to me if you really need it. I just love you, Charlie. That's all. And I would do anything for you. I want to be there for you, but only if you let me."

I closed my eyes and it was like the words just sort of fell out, "I'm gonna visit my father."

She immediately began to cough on her food. "Excuse me?"

"My father," I said again. "My friends are picking me up this afternoon and we're gonna go see him."

"Are… are you sure about this?"

"No."

"Well, then maybe you shouldn't go."

"I have to."

"You don't have to do anything, honey. This is entirely up to you."

I dropped my hands to the table and sighed. "It's hard to explain, but just trust me on this. I have to go."

"For closure?"

I opened my mouth and closed it suddenly. "Yeah, closure."

It felt like centuries had passed as she looked me up and down. Finally, she placed a hand on mine and smiled.

"Well then," she said. "I guess you've got it all figured out. Just promise me you'll check in with me after you get home so I know you're okay?"

I nodded.

She smiled and gave my hand one last squeeze before going back to her breakfast. It felt good being honest with her, almost like a weight had been lifted from my shoulders. It also made this whole thing feel all the more real. I was doing this. I was *actually* going to see my father. I grabbed my fork and knife and forced down a few bites of food; if I was really doing this, then I was going to need all the energy I could get.

I spent the rest of the afternoon eyeing the clock until Scotty's huge white truck finally pulled into the driveway. My stomach immediately swelled with nerves, and for a brief second, I actually considered calling the whole thing off. But then Scotty honked his horn, and I snapped back to my senses. This was happening. Without wasting another second, I forced myself to my feet and out the front door. As soon I climbed into the backseat of Scotty's truck, he looked at me and scowled.

"Well you look like shit," he said.

"Nice to see you too," I mumbled.

"Seriously," he said. "You look like you're going to be sick. If you puke in my truck, there will be hell to pay."

"Oh leave him alone," Andy said from the front passenger seat.

"Leave him *alone*?" He scoffed. "For your information, this is a classic 1978 Jeep Honcho with all the proper supernatural enhancements. I got it from my uncle after he passed. If you think I'm going to trust Charlie's weak stomach with the original leather interior, you're insane."

"I'm not gonna puke," I snapped. "Can we just get on the road already? I wanna get this over with."

"Fine," Scotty said, turning back in his seat. "But if you yak, you're cleaning it up."

"Whatever," I muttered.

He shifted gears, and the car lurched. Just like that, we were off.

For the most part, it was a quiet ride. I kept my window open a crack so a light breeze blew through my hair. It definitely helped with the nerves. Eventually, the brick storefronts turned to long stretches of country highway and endless corn fields; rural Virginia was truly a beautiful place. It was peaceful; relaxing even. For a brief moment, I even thought I might actually have my anxiety in check, but then we drove past the welcome sign for the town of Ladysmith and the panic returned. It only seemed to grow worse when we pulled up to the hospital.

When the car finally came to a stop, the others got out of the truck, but not me. I stayed put. I was totally frozen stiff as I stared at that faded brick building, the words *Ladysmith Mental Health* in big gray letters above the entrance. Everything looked worn and dull as if it had been forgotten for years. The grass was overgrown, the chain linked fence that surrounded the parking lot rusted. Even the cars parked in the lot were older and broken down. I must've been sitting there for a long while because eventually the side door popped open, and Andy stood in front of me.

"You okay?" she asked.

Before I could answer, Scotty shouted, "I didn't drive four hours to hang out in a parking lot, you know!"

"Chill out!" she yelled back over her shoulder before hopping in the seat next to me and closing the door. "All right, let's cut the bullshit. Tell me what's on your mind."

I rubbed my hands over my face and sighed. "I just don't know if I can do this."

"Why not?"

"Because, I'm *me*."

"Yeah, and you're amazing."

"No I'm not," I mumbled. "You just don't get it."

"Sure I do."

"No," I said. "You really don't. I'm *terrified* of my father. It's really pathetic, I know. He's stronger than me, and he's definitely smarter. I'm worthless compared to him. Always will be."

"That's not true," she said.

"Yeah, it—"

"No," she stated firmly. "Listen, I'm sorry you had to grow up with that monster, but you are not a victim. You're a *survivor,* Charlie. Never forget that. You survived, and you're stronger than you think. Despite what he did to you, you've become the most caring, selfless, and loyal person I've ever met, while your father is nothing but a broken old man that beat up on a little kid. But you're not a little kid anymore, all right? And I have no doubt in my mind you can do this."

There was a moment of silence as she looked at me with a burning passion in her eyes. Those were the exact words I needed to hear. It lit a fire under my ass.

"Thanks," I said softly.

"Are you gonna be okay?"

"I think so."

She grinned. "Good, because I think Scotty might go off the deep end if you back out now."

I let out a weak laugh.

"So, you ready to go?"

"Yeah," I said, taking a deep breath. "Let's do this."

As we climbed out of the car, I noticed Scotty had been pacing back and forth, his lips pressed tight into a thin white line. He immediately started complaining about us taking forever, but I ignored him and marched right through the front door and into the foyer. The tile floors were ashen and yellow, the white brick walls cold and sterile. Andy yanked on the door that lead to the lobby, but it didn't budge. Instead, a woman's voice came from a small intercom speaker next to it.

"Ladysmith Mental Health," she said. "How may I help you?"

"Oh, erm…." I glanced at my friends and raised my eyebrow. "We're here for a visit."

"And what's your name?" she asked.

"Charlie Stewart," I said.

"Good, and how about the patient's name?"

"Allan Stewart." "What's the relation?"

"He's…" I paused as a sense of disgust brewed in the pit of my stomach. "He's my father."

There were sounds of scribbling. "Did you schedule ahead of time?"

My eyes grew wide. "I didn't know we had to."

She chuckled. "Don't worry about it. We'll have to make sure your father is available for visits this afternoon, but it shouldn't be a problem. Just sit tight in the waiting room while I go check on him."

The door buzzed, and Andy pushed it open. When I walked in, I wasn't at all surprised to find the lobby was just as worn as the rest of the building. There were leather couches surrounding a chipped, wooden table that had a stack of outdated health magazines on top of it. I looked around at the endless collection of motivational posters and cheap motel art hanging on the walls before easing myself into a particularly stiff arm chair. And then I waited. It was oddly quiet; the only sound was that of a large grandfather clock stowed away in the corner. I counted each and every tick one by one. I must've counted to a thousand or more before a short, plump nurse with bright red lips walked into the room. When she approached me, my heart beat in my throat.

"Charlie?" she asked.

"That's me," I said.

"Wonderful," she said. "I have great news. Your father's able to take visitors today. He's in the recreational room just down the hall." She glanced at my friends. "Are all three of you visiting?"

"Yeah, if that's okay," I said.

"Sure," she said. "Whenever you're ready, I'll take you over."

I looked to Andy, and she gave me a reassuring nod. No turning back now. I followed the woman down the long and winding hallway, holding my breath as we went around each and every corner. Finally, the hall opened to a large, rectangular room that smelled strongly of Pine-sol and cigarettes. It was dark and dingy with very few windows, wood paneled walls, and beige tile floors. I noticed a television stationed to some old cartoon playing in one corner. Across the way was a pool table as well as a handful of men crouched over a game of cards. It seemed all the patients wore this beige jumpsuit while the orderlies were dressed in white. The record player was on low and playing classical piano, but nobody seemed to be paying it any attention.

"He's been doing quite well these past few weeks," the nurse said. "But I do want to warn you that because of his violent offense, he's going to have to be hand-cuffed to the table. Is that all right?"

"It's fine," I said.

"Good." She nodded over my shoulder toward the back of the room. "He's just over there. We have a few orderlies present to keep an eye on things, so if you need anything, just ask them."

I nodded.

Her lips curled. "I'll leave you to it then. Have fun."

Have *fun*.

She walked off, and it wasn't until she disappeared around the corner that I finally mustered the courage to look across the room. As soon as my eyes laid on him, my stomach hitched. His back might've been to me, but I knew it was him; there was no mistaking it. He was sitting on a dark green couch, his wrists shackled to the table as the nurse had promised. I must've been staring for a while because eventually, Andy nudged me. This was it. I forced one foot in front of the other, each step sending my heart into spasm. It was almost an out of body experience until I finally stopped in front of him.

This man.

This *shell* of a man was my father.

His hair was longer than I'd remembered, his skin dull with dark bags under his eyes. His once full face was now gaunt and hollow as if he hadn't eaten for months. He wore the same dirty beige jumpsuit as the other patients as well as scuffed brown shoes and a blue, long sleeved undershirt that was stained and withered. Poking out from behind the metal handcuffs was a thick, jagged scar on his wrist. As I looked him over, I realized he had absolutely no life behind his eyes. None at all. He didn't even seem to register that I was there and just stared at the small, wooden coffee table between us as if he were asleep with his eyes open. It was then that I started to wonder how the hell I was ever so scared of him. Andy was right; he was nothing more than a broken old man. With that thought in mind, I felt a slight bout of confidence and eased onto the couch across from him while Andy sat next to me. Scotty took the metal folding chair to our left, and before I could even say a word, he leaned toward my father with an eager smile and stuck out his hand.

"It's a pleasure to meet you, sir," he said.

My father didn't move. In fact, I wasn't even sure he was breathing. It was like all the lights were on, but no one was home. After a moment, Scotty lowered his hand, and his smile faded.

"Right," he said. "Well, we're running on a tight schedule, so I guess we'll just get right to it then. I wanted to ask you some questions about a book you once had in your possession. One that details the true origins of the four horsemen of the apocalypse. Does that ring any bells?"

Silence.

He narrowed his eyes. "Sir?"

Still nothing.

Scotty finally turned to me and scoffed. "Does he talk?"

I shrugged.

"Do something," he snapped.

"Like what?" I asked.

"I don't know, *anything*," he said. "He's your father. Maybe he'll talk to you."

With gritted teeth, I forced myself to look at his cold blue eyes; I'd never forget them. For a while, the words were caught in my throat, but I eventually got them out.

"So, uh, that book that Scotty mentioned," I said, uncomfortably rubbing the back of my neck. "Someone has a copy or stole yours or something, and now we think they're using it to break the four seals to release the horsemen. We're at a complete loss and could really use some help."

I sat on the edge of my seat and waited for any indication that he knew what I was talking about or that he even *heard* me, but there was nothing. He just stared at that damn coffee table as if I wasn't even in the room. My blood boiled. The longer I sat there, the more the anger spread throughout my body. It reached the very tips of my fingers and toes until I exploded like a firework and banged my fist on the table.

"Wake the hell up!" I shouted.

"Calm down," Andy said, grabbing my shoulder.

"No," I said, brushing her hand away. "I knew it was a mistake to come here. He wasn't gonna help me. He'd never help me. He *hates* me. This whole thing was a waste of time. Come on, let's go."

I made a move to stand, but then I heard it—the sound of metal clattering. It was his cuffs jangling as he opened and closed his hands. It was then I noticed his lips part, and my heart skipped a beat.

He mumbled something, but his voice was barely a hoarse whisper.

"Excuse me?" Scotty asked.

"Don't..." He cleared his throat. "Don't go. Please."

I couldn't believe it. He spoke. He actually *spoke*. It looked so painful for him to choke out those few words, and for a brief moment, I actually felt sorry for him, but that didn't last all that long. This was my father, after all. He wasn't sorry; he'd never be.

"Start talking or we're out of here," I snapped.

"I promised her," he whispered.

"Huh?"

"I promised her I'd take care of you," he said a bit louder.

"Who?" I asked.

It was as if he didn't even hear me as he looked at the scars on his wrists. "I'm so sorry, Nadine."

I was at a complete loss for words. After everything that'd happened, he was apologizing to my mother. Not me. It was abundantly clear that he couldn't give less of a crap about me. It was the final straw, and something in me snapped.

"You promised her you'd *protect* me?" I asked, my voice shaking. "That's a fucking joke."

"Charlie," Andy said softly.

I ignored her, my seething gaze fixated on my father. "You broke that promise the day she died. All those cigarettes you put out on me. The times you held my head under water until I blacked out. What would she think of that? The one thing I don't think I'll ever understand is why you didn't just kill me when I was a kid. Why'd you have to wait seventeen goddamn years to do it?"

He remained silent, his eyes brimming with tears, but I didn't care. I wanted the words to hurt. I wanted them to *kill* him. After a moment, he raised his gaze to meet mine for the first time.

"I couldn't do it," he whispered.

"Why the hell not?"

"Your eyes." He blinked, and a tear rolled down his face. "You… you have your mother's eyes."

I clenched my fists so tight they shook. "Yeah, well too bad you're never gonna see them again."

With that, I marched off before he could say another word. It wasn't until I reached the hallway that a piercing scream caused me to stop. I spun around to find my father on his feet, screaming at the top of his lungs and yanking at his handcuffs. He kicked over the metal folding chair just as the orderlies wrapped their arms around him, but there was no stopping him. He was losing his mind, shoving them away and yanking at the cuffs until his wrists bled. When they finally got a good hand on him, they dragged him into a back room. As they reached the door, his eyes locked with mine.

"The war," he shouted. "It's already begun. The first seal was broken with Venator blood, as will the last. Radar, Charlie. If you find him, you'll find the book."

As they finally pulled him through the door, I could hear his voice trailing off until it disappeared completely. I stood in stunned silence for the longest time until Scotty snatched my arm and we jetted out of there. It wasn't until we piled into his truck and locked the doors that he finally spoke.

"Holy crap," he said, gripping the steering wheel in disbelief. "Do you guys know what this means?"

"What?" I asked.

"You heard him," he said. "The war has begun. Everything we've suspected: it's true. It's all true. Christ, we better hurry home and do some research."

"That's gonna have to wait until tomorrow," Andy said. "Mick changes tonight, remember?"

"You've got to be joking," he mumbled.

"No, I'm not," she said. "And since I'm the one with the tranquilizers, we should probably get a move on."

"*You* have the tranquilizers?" he asked.

"Sure do," she said. "They're in my backpack."

He rolled his eyes and scoffed. "Unbelievable. You three are the most irresponsible people I've ever met."

"Just shut up and hit the road," she snapped.

"Yeah, yeah," he muttered as he shifted the car into gear.

The ride home felt much quicker than the one to the hospital. I just had so much to process, it made my head hurt. In fact, I wasn't sure I'd be of much help with Mick. I was way too distracted. One thing was for sure, I wanted to talk with Edgar once we got back; he'd be able to help sort out my thoughts. When we finally pulled into my driveway, the sun was just starting its descent over the horizon. Just as the truck came to a stop, Andy glanced at her watch and shook her head.

"I still don't see why you couldn't just drop us off at Mick's," she said.

"It's for his own good," Scotty said. "If I knew where he lived, I wouldn't be able to resist the hunt."

"You're ridiculous," Andy said.

"No," he said. "I'm what you'd call *responsible.*"

"It's fine," I said, unbuckling my seatbelt. "I wanted to talk with Edgar before we go anyway."

"We don't have time," Andy said.

"It'll be quick," I said. "Promise."

She chewed her lip and looked me over before finally heaving a sigh. "Fine, but fifteen minutes *tops.*"

"No problem," I said.

Scotty opened his car door and hopped out. "I'm going with Charlie. I want to meet this Edgar character."

As I reached for the car door handle, a thought popped into my head that caused my stomach to drop. Before I got out, I looked at Andy and furrowed my brow.

"Hey, do you think you could do me a favor?" I asked.

"Sure," she said.

"I promised my aunt I'd tell her when I got back," I said. "Could you swing by and let her know I'm okay?"

"Yeah, no problem," she said.

"Thanks," I said. "I'll meet you there after, and then we can head over to Mick's together."

With the plan set, we got out of the car and went our separate ways. Scotty and I started up Edgar's driveway just as Andy disappeared through my aunt's garage. When we approached the front door, I held my breath and knocked. Almost immediately, it swung open, and Edgar stood before us. There was a beat of silence as he looked from Scotty to me, an eager smile growing on his face.

"Did you see him?" he asked.

I nodded.

His smile spread even wider before he turned to Scotty. "And I take it you must be Scotty?"

"How'd you know?" Scotty asked.

"Charlie's told me so much about you," he said.

Scotty grunted. "Likewise."

Edgar pushed the door open and stepped aside. "Come on in. I'll grab you two something to drink, and then you can tell me all about it."

We walked past him and into the living room where I plopped down on the couch. Edgar made his way into the kitchen, which Scotty took as an opportunity to inspect the place. He began grabbing trinkets from the fireplace mantle and turning them over in his hand as if they had some sort of magic to them before shaking his head and placing them back. I rolled my eyes as he started to search beneath the couch, and then Edgar returned with two glasses of water. Scotty threw himself next to me just as Edgar handed us the drinks and sat in the armchair across from us.

"So, tell me everything," Edgar said. "How did he look?"

"Different," I said. "I don't know, it was weird. It was him, but at the same time, it wasn't. He was way skinnier and pale, almost as if he was sick or something. He just seemed so out of it."

"Did you stand up to him?" he asked.

"I guess," I said, tracing the rim of my glass. "It just wasn't what I expected. I couldn't help but feel bad for him."

"Don't," Edgar said. "I mean it, Charlie. Allan does *not* deserve your sympathy."

"Yeah, I know," I mumbled.

"Please," he pressed on. "Tell me more. Did he say anything?"

"Yeah," I said. "There was something about the war having already begun, and how it starts and ends with Venator blood. He also mentioned something about a guy named Radar. He told us if we found Radar, then we'd find the book, but I don't know. None of it makes any sense."

His eyes grew wide. "Radar?"

"Yeah," I said.

"Does that name mean anything to you?" Scotty piped up.

"Yes, actually." He began to stroke his chin. "In fact, I know Radar quite well."

I frowned. "You *do*?"

Scotty moved to the edge of his seat. "Where can we find him?"

Edgar chuckled. "Patience young man. First, I'd like to ask Charlie here a few more questions."

"We don't have time for that," Scotty said.

"Oh, I can assure you, we do." He turned back to me, a peculiar grin etched across his face. "Tell me, Charlie. Did Allan look at all terrified at the thought of the horsemen being let loose?"

I raised my eyebrow. "Umm, I guess, but what—"

"Or perhaps he teared up," he continued, his eyes sparkling with excitement. "That would've been fantastic to witness first hand. Allan reduced to tears like the sniveling coward he is."

I blinked a few times, totally dumbfounded as to what the hell he was talking about. I started to think maybe he was just projecting his hatred of his own father onto mine, but then something strange occurred to me, and my stomach dropped. The longer I thought about it, the harder my gut twisted until I thought I might throw up. I finally looked to Edgar, my heart beating in my throat.

"You know his name," I whispered.

"Excuse me?"

"His name," I said a bit louder. "You keep saying it. *Allan*. But how would you know that?"

He let out a soft laugh. "You told me, of course."

"No I didn't," I replied.

"Sure, you did," he said. "Just the other day you—"

"No, I *didn't*," I stated firmly.

Just then, Scotty dropped his glass of water, and it shattered to pieces all over the wood floor. He clutched his throat and began to cough. At the same time his skin grew pale, and little beads of sweat formed on his brow. Before I knew it, he collapsed to the floor, and I rushed to his side.

I began frantically shaking his arm. "Scotty, wake up!"

"He can't hear you," Edgar said.

It was then that I looked up and a breath caught in my lungs. Staring me down was the wrong end of a silver pistol. I froze, my chest compressed so tight I could hardly breathe. Edgar on the other hand appeared to be calm, cheerful even. His hand was as still as stone as he pointed the gun in my face. There was a fire in his eyes, one that made him look like an entirely different person.

"I think you and I need to have a little chat," he said.

"Who are you?" I asked.

His lip curled into a sinister grin. "Oh, Charlie, it seems you and I have a lot more in common than you think."

With his gun pointed at me, Edgar rushed to the window and closed the drapes. He pulled out a stack of ropes from a nearby coat closet and instructed me to sit at the wooden chair and place my hands behind my back while he tied me up. The entire time, I fought the urge to cry. I just felt so damn stupid. Edgar. I'd opened up to him. I *told* him things I'd never told anyone before, and look where it got me. I glanced at Scotty who was still passed out cold on the floor. I noticed the place on his forehead where he'd hit the ground was already starting to swell, but at least he was breathing.

When Edgar finally finished tying my hands, he walked around and sat on the coffee table across from me. I kept my gaze locked on the floor. I just couldn't bring myself to look at him.

"I trusted you," I said finally.

"Yes," he replied, "but I promise, that was no mistake. You have to understand; I don't want to hurt you."

"Then what's going on?"

"I've said it before, Charlie, you and I have a lot more in common than you think."

"No, we don't," I said, my tone sharp.

"Oh, but we do. In fact, we share the same blood."

For the first time, my eyes flicked up to meet his. His dark stare was burning with such intensity, it felt as though he could look right through me and into my soul. It was then that I remembered he'd known my father's name. I took a shaky breath, my heart pounding so hard it hurt.

"Who are you?" I asked.

"Come on, Charlie," he said. "I thought you were smarter than that. Surely you've figured it out by now."

I closed my eyes and swallowed. "You're Radar, aren't you?"

He grinned. "Yes, now you're getting it. Radar was this stupid little nickname Allan had given me when we were growing up. I always used to be the one stuck on lookout whenever we'd sneak around our father's back."

"*Our* father?" I paused, my throat growing tight. "But that means..."

He nodded. "Not only are Allan and I brothers, we shared the same womb. We're twins, Charlie."

I stared in shock, a breath hitched in my lungs. His brother. His *twin*. So many questions raced through my mind, but I couldn't seem to get a grasp on one. Instead, I gawked like an idiot until he finally got to his feet and began to pace in front of me, his lips twisted into a peculiar grin.

"Yes," he said, "But even though we are brothers, we couldn't be more different. We even *looked* different. He was always the handsome one. The charming one. I, on the other hand, was quiet and introverted. While he had a passion for hunting creatures, I preferred to read about them. Despite these differences, we got along well enough, but there was always one thing we seemed to disagree on." He stopped and turned to me. "Your father was brainwashed, Charlie. He was so damn excited to see the world. To go on adventures. It didn't matter that our own father was an abusive alcoholic, he wanted to be just like him. Yes, it seemed being a Venator was in Allan's blood—but not mine." He continued pacing, though at this point, his smile was gone. "One day when we were fourteen years old, Allan disappeared. No word. No note. Nothing. He abandoned me and left me to die with that wretched man who called himself our father. It was clear Allan never cared about me. He was just like the rest of them. *Venators.* God, they're the worst sorts of creatures. Selfish. Violent. Uncivilized. The world is better off without them. They *deserve* this."

"Deserve what?" I asked.

"The horsemen," he said, his smile returning. "Now, there's something I must come clean about, Charlie. I hope you're not upset, but it seems I might've lied to you the other day. It was necessary though, I promise. You see, when I'd mentioned the entire race of Venators being affected by this curse, that's not really the case. Not at all. In fact, it really only affects one bloodline. *Ours.*"

Edgar sat back on the coffee table, his elbows resting on his knees. He leaned forward, his dark glare searing into me.

"I'm going to tell you a little story, Charlie," he said. "Back before the second world war, there was talk of a powerful book, one that had the ability to bring about the apocalypse. For the longest time, no one knew it's whereabouts and it remained nothing more than an old wives' tale—that is, until the first seal was broken. Panic spread like wildfire all throughout the supernatural world. It wasn't until a Venator by the name of Arthur Grimsly discovered the book that the world calmed. He became the book's protector, however, in doing so, he placed a curse upon his family which doomed any woman carrying Grimsly blood in her womb to die in childbirth while the father would succumb to a fierce rage and was destined to murder the child. It was this sacrifice that returned the world to peace. It also led to a man hunt. Every dark creature in existence wanted Arthur's head on a stick. It became far too dangerous to reveal his true identity, so he changed it and went into hiding." He paused and took a breath. "If you haven't already guessed, Arthur Grimsly was my father. Grimsly is my true last name, as it is yours. Allan and I spent our entire lives traveling with our father and hiding our identities in order to keep that book safe."

I looked to the floor, my chest so tight, I could hardly breathe. Grimsly. That was my real name. I just couldn't wrap my head around it. It was then that I realized something, and I looked to Edgar.

"How'd my father end up with it?" I asked.

"The book?"

I nodded.

He folded his hands in his lap. "Well, when Allan ran away, he took it upon himself to steal the book from my father and take it with him. I imagine he believed my father wasn't in the right frame of mind. And he wasn't wrong; my father was a complete dunce and absolutely out of his mind at that point in his life. I also believe that Allan didn't trust me. As much as I hate to admit it, that was quite smart of him. He *shouldn't* have trusted me. You see, shortly after I turned twenty, I murdered my father and have been in search for Allan ever since. It's been my life's mission to steal the book back and finish what was started."

As he finished speaking, a blanket of silence fell over us. I refused to look at him and instead kept my gaze locked on the floor, my mind racing with so many thoughts. After a moment, he sighed.

"I know it's a lot to take in," he said," but you have to trust me."

"*Trust* you?"

"Yes, don't you see, Charlie? I'm not the bad guy. Venators are. Just take one look at their bloody history and you'll soon discover they're mindless, killing machines. Murderers. *Animal*s. God, all this violence and pain…" He dug his fingers into his hair and raised his voice. "It's absolutely barbaric, Charlie! It's poisonous! I want them dead. All of them." He took a deep breath and gathered himself before looking at me with a mischievous grin. "That is, except for you."

"Me?"

"You know, it's funny because I originally thought you'd be just like them. Just as wicked and brutish. You were Allan's son, after all. Ever since I came about Allan's whereabouts, I had planned to use your blood to break the last seal. I thought it'd be poetic. My own brother's son, the final sacrifice that brought about the apocalypse. In fact, that night you were poking around my basement was going to be *the* night. I'd even went so far as to poison your water, but then I learned you were like me. Abused. Full of anger. A victim of this horrific curse. You hated your father just as much as I hated my own. I could hear it in your voice. The way you spoke of him. In that moment, I knew you were just like me, and in time I'd be able to convince you of my ways. I no longer wanted to hurt you; I wanted you to join me. I still do. You and I are going to finish this together. I just need you to understand."

He got to his feet and headed to the kitchen. I could hear him rummaging around, and before long, he was back with what looked like a metal gurney covered in a plastic sheet and a blue mop bucket filled with a bunch of random tools. I could see a screwdriver, and a hammer, as well as a small axe.

I watched curiously as he spread out a sheet of plastic wrap all around the room. I had no idea what the hell he was doing, until finally he approached Scotty's limp body and hoisted him onto the gurney. Suddenly, it clicked. The blood of a Venator. I snapped back to reality and began squirming beneath my ropes.

"Hold on," I said. "Scotty's not a Venator. He's …"

I closed my eyes and wondered how on earth I was going to explain that Scotty wasn't a Venator when he lived and breathed the supernatural world. Hell, the kid even dressed like Van Helsing.

"Just trust me," I finally said. "He's not one of them."

"Don't lie to me," Edgar snapped.

"I'm not lying," I said, the panic in my voice growing. "I swear. You're making a huge mistake."

He ignored me and continued to wrap a string of rope around Scotty's chest and arms so he was secure. He then grabbed a sharp pair of scissors and a sense of dread filled me as I thought the worst, but instead he simply sliced through Scotty's shirt. When he finally cut through the sleeve on his left wrist, he lit up.

"There it is," he said. "The mark of a Venator."

"That's…" I closed my eyes and let out a deep sigh. "That's not what it looks like."

His eyes snapped to mine. "Stop defending him. I know you think he's your friend, but he's not. He's the enemy."

I cursed beneath my breath and began to writhe around, doing anything I could to break free, but the ropes were so tight that even the slightest movement sent a sharp pain through arms. I fought through it, my heart hammering in my chest as Edgar leaned over Scotty's body and gave his face a light tap. He did it harder and harder until finally Scotty began to stir. As he opened his eyes, he looked around the room, though he was clearly still in a daze. His eyelids were fluttering, and his skin pale. It wasn't until he realized that he was strapped to a gurney that he really seemed to wake up.

"Why can't I move?" he asked.

"Exactophine," Edgar said. "It's the sedative I placed in your water. It works quite fast and renders its victims immobile for several hours. But don't worry, this won't take nearly that long."

"What the hell is going on?" he asked, the panic in his voice rising.

Edgar smiled and placed a strip of duct tape over Scotty's mouth. "You'll see soon enough."

Scotty's eyes grew wide with terror. He began to scream, but what came out was nothing more than a muffled groan. I began twisting and turning harder and more urgently as I watched Edgar rummage through the bucket. It seemed he was toying with Scotty, grabbing one and dangling it over Scotty's face with a demented smile, only to frown and shake his head before putting it back to pick another. Before long, Scotty's hair was matted to his head in sweat, his body shaking more violently with each tool's glimmer. He continued to shout, but with the duct tape over his mouth, he only mumbled. Finally, Edgar pulled out a large butcher knife and held it inches from Scotty's face.

"You're making a mistake," I said, still struggling against my ropes. "I'm telling you, he's *not* a Venator!"

"Be quiet," Edgar snapped.

For the first time, I noticed a book on the lower shelf of the gurney. It was thick, the cover a worn shade of red, and the pages decayed to a dirty brown. I finally realized just what it was and gasped. It was the book I'd snuck from my father's private stash and read so many years ago. The four horsemen. Edgar took it from the bottom shelf and placed it so it was just below Scotty's left arm before leaning over his body with a sinister grin.

"The last seal," he said, his voice a low growl. "God, I've been waiting for this day for so long. Now, I'm going to let you in on a little secret. In order to break this seal, I need blood. *Venator* blood. The only problem is, I'm not quite sure just how much I'll need, so I figured we'd start small and work our way up until every last drop of your blood is spilled onto those pages. And don't you worry, I promise I'll make this as painful as possible."

I held my breath as Edgar rested the knife against Scotty's face and began to drag it gently across his skin. Down his cheek and to his chin. He continued over his neck and chest, and then back up again. Scotty closed his eyes, his chest rising and falling at a rapid pace. At this point, I was tugging so hard at my ropes, my entire chair was rocking and my skin burned from the deep cuts.

Edgar moved so close to Scotty's face, their noses nearly touched. The look in Edgar's eye was one of pure malice. From across the room, I could hear Scotty's shallow breaths and could even see the beads of sweat as they rolled down the sides of his face. Edgar seemed to relish in his fear until finally, his lip curled.

"Are you scared?" he asked.

"Please!" I shouted as a pathetic last attempt to stop him, but it was no use. He ignored me and raised the butcher knife high into the air.

"I sure hope so," he hissed.

The moment seemed to last forever as he held the knife over his head, the light reflecting off the shiny metal. And then in one quick move, he brought it down onto Scotty's arm, slicing right over his tattoo. The dull thud as the blade cut through skin and hit his bone was like nothing I'd ever heard before. I wanted to faint or vomit, but instead I remained frozen in fear and watched as Edgar raised the knife up and brought it down again and again. I could hear Scotty's blood curdling screams muffled behind the duct tape, but worst of all was the sound the knife made once it finally cut clean through Scotty's arm and connected with the metal gurney beneath him. I forced myself to look at the bloody gashes that were all up and down Scotty's arm from missed swings, as well as the little bits of skin that flapped back and forth as blood poured from his wound. Next to him was his dead hand, the skin a sickly shade of white. Edgar watched with fire in his eyes as the blood dripped to the book below, but before anything could happen, the doorbell rang.

I gasped and turned my head as far as it could go. Until that moment, I'd completely forgotten the outside world even existed, but once my memories came rushing back, I thought of Andy. I told her we'd be fifteen minutes tops. When I looked back to Edgar, the gun was already pointed at me.

"Are you expecting anyone?" he asked.

"No," I said quickly.

"Don't lie to me."

"I'm not. Whoever it is, I-I'm sure they'll go away."

He narrowed his eyes as he looked to the door. Inside, I was screaming at the top of my lungs for Andy to run away. Get help. *Anything*. But I knew she couldn't hear me. The only thing I could do was hope to god Edgar would forget about it and let her go so she'd be safe. But then the doorbell rang again, and my heart sank. Before I could say another word, Edgar began to clumsily wrap a bandage and a tight band around Scotty's arm to stop the blood.

"Don't think I wasn't watching you," he said over his shoulder.

"Huh?" I asked.

"It's that girl, isn't it? The one you were with earlier?"

I pressed my lips shut and stayed quiet, my only defense. The moment seemed to last forever as he finished tying the band on Scotty's arm. Finally, he grabbed his gun and strutted past me.

"Scream, and I'll blow her brains out," he said.

It was useless. *I* was useless. I closed my eyes in defeat and listened to Andy's whimpers as Edgar dragged her into the living room and threw her to the floor at the opposite side of the room from me. Her eyes grew wide in horror when she spotted Scotty passed out on the gurney all bloodied up. She looked all around the room to the blood-stained book that still rested on the floor, as well as the rusted bucket filled with sharp tools. When she finally noticed me, she perked up.

"Charlie," she said.

"No talking," Edgar snapped.

"W-what's going on?" she asked.

"I said *quiet*," he said, his voice raised. "On the ground and put your hands behind your head. If you so much as move an inch, I swear, I will put a bullet through your skull without thinking twice."

She swallowed hard and slowly moved her hands behind her head. Edgar smirked at her obedience before turning his attention back to Scotty. By this point, Scotty's skin was a sickly shade of white, and his breaths were sharp and sporadic. His forehead was drenched in sweat with little beads pouring down the side of his face. At that moment, I felt so damn hopeless. Like, there was nothing I could do to help him. Or *Andy* for the matter. We were screwed. All of us, and it was my fault. For bringing them to Edgar's place. For being dumb enough to trust him. I felt like a complete and total idiot. The only thing I could do was hope Aunt Joy wouldn't come looking for me. At least she could be spared if she just did what everyone else should've done and forgot about me. I looked to Andy once more, my heart squeezing with guilt. She was staring at the ground, her entire body trembling so hard,

I could hear the zipper on her backpack jingling against the purple nylon material. It was then that it hit me and a little glimmer of hope sparked back into me.

"I'm sorry," I called over to Andy. "This is all my fault."

"Don't say that," she said softly.

"It's true though. If it weren't for me, you'd be over at Mick's right now playing *darts*."

She frowned. "Huh?"

I took a deep breath and raised my voice. "You were always the best at *darts*; you never miss."

"Enough talking!" Edgar shouted.

He crouched down and began running his fingers over the blood stained pages of the book.

I kept my gaze locked on Andy and hoped like hell she was picking up on what I was trying to say. She looked back to me, her brow scrunched in confusion, and I strained my eyes, doing everything I could to communicate to her without speaking a word. She just had to understand. The tranquilizers in her bag. If I could find a way to distract Edgar, she could use one on him.

"Dammit," Edgar said. "Why isn't this working?"

"I already told you," I said, tearing my eyes away from her. "Scotty's not a Venator."

"That can't be."

"Well, it is. Face it, your plan failed."

He clenched his jaw and glared at me. I did my best to appear calm and collected, but it was hard to forget about the large pistol in his hand. After a moment, he let out a frustrated breath.

"Why're you behaving like this, Charlie?" he asked. "You and I. We're supposed to be a team."

"Well we're not," I said.

"I'm doing this for us. For *revenge*. You think you'd be more grateful."

"You don't care about me. You're just using me for your own petty revenge against my father. I get that you're angry. I'm angry, too. What your dad did to you… it was unforgivable. But it doesn't have to come to this. I know sometimes it might feel like the world did you wrong, but you can't let anger control your life. You need to find peace with what happened and move on."

His expression softened. "You know, I really do care about you, Charlie."

"Then let us go."

"I can't."

"But you—"

"I'm going to ask you one last time, are you with me or not?"

I lowered my chin to my chest and sighed. "I'm not."

He stared at me longingly a moment before his angry sneer returned. "Well then, it seems I'm in need of Venator blood, and for whatever reason, Scotty's is not making the cut. If you're not on my side, then I guess your blood is going to have to do."

He snatched the bloody knife from the gurney and lunged at me, but a clatter from across the room caused him to stop dead in his tracks. We both turned to find Andy, frozen in fear as a stack of cassettes spilled from her backpack. In her hand was the tranquilizer gun with the dart already loaded. As soon as Edgar spotted it, he jerked his gun at her, and the next thing I knew, there was a loud bang. I immediately closed my eyes as the deafening sound reverberated through the room. It was so loud, it felt as though my head was split in two. When I finally opened my eyes, Andy and Edgar were both on the floor. My heart beat like a snare drum, and I began tugging at my restraints harder than ever.

It was then that I noticed the dart in Edgar's chest as he writhed around. For a while, he was stuck in a daze before pulling it from himself and tossing it aside. He gasped for air as he crawled toward the book, his body just starting to convulse. Before I could do much of anything, he grabbed the knife and used it to slit his wrists. With his final breath, he laid his bloodied arm over the pages of the book before falling unconscious.

Almost at once, an eerie chill filled the room, causing the hair on my neck to stand on end. For the first time, I stopped tugging at the ropes and sat as still as stone. A floorboard creaked behind me, but when I looked over my shoulder, there was nothing there. I heard it again, only this time it was closer. Closer. *Closer.* Suddenly sparks began shooting from the book. My body jolted, and I watched in shock as a burst of black flames shot from the pages. In no time at all, the sparks caught fire to the curtains and a thick black smoke filled the air. As hard as it was, I tore my focus from the growing fire and looked across the room to find Andy on her back. She was clutching her bicep and groaning in agony, but at least she was alive.

"Andy!" I shouted. "Are you okay?"

"Yeah, I think so," she said through gritted teeth. "It's just my arm. That bastard shot me!"

"He what?"

"I'll be fine," she said, adding under her breath, "Shit, this hurts."

"Quick," I said. "Come untie me. We need to get out of here before this place burns to the ground."

She took a pained breath before hobbling over and undoing my restraints. When I was free, I grimaced and rubbed my hands over my

forearms which were bloody and red from the rope. My lungs filled
with smoke as I looked around the room I realized the flames were now
spread all around us and growing by the second. I hardly even had time
to look at Edgar's lifeless body as Andy and I undid Scotty's restraints.
His skin was so pale; it was clear he was barely holding on. Right
before we hoisted him up, I grabbed Andy's backpack and swung it
over my shoulder, and from there, we dragged Scotty toward the front
door. The smoke was so thick; it was nearly impossible to see where I
was going. With each step, I coughed harder and harder until my lungs
were on fire. When we finally made it outside, the three of us sprawled
onto the dewy grass.

God, the air never tasted so fresh. I drew in each breath and held it
a long second before slowly letting it out. When I finally calmed, I sat
up and watched in awe as Edgar's place succumbed to the fire. I
couldn't help but think of the theatre fire, and the beautiful yet
terrifying way the flames cackled and sent wisps of smoke to drift
toward the night sky and wrap around the glowing moon.

The full moon.

Mick.

As happy as I was that we'd made it out alive, I knew this wasn't
quite over; we had to act fast. I snatched Andy's backpack and dug
around for the second tranquilizer. For a while I worried she hadn't
packed one, but then I wrapped my hands around the thin metal barrel
and let out a sigh of relief. That relief faded once I realized Andy had
left the gun in Edgar's house. I looked to the fire, a lump growing in
my throat as I began to realize just what I'd have to do—I was going to
have to use the tranquilizer by hand. As in, stand within arm's reach of
a fully grown werewolf and stab him with a dart. I didn't really even
have time to fully process this, so I did my best to put on a brave face

and turned to Andy who was still lying on her back and clutching at her shoulder.

"Call an ambulance," I said as I climbed to my feet.

"Where are you going?" she asked.

"I need to get Mick his tranquilizer."

"No way you're going without me. I'm always the one who shoots him."

She started to stand, but I stuck out my hand. "You and Scotty both need serious medical attention."

"Yeah, but—"

"Don't worry about me. Besides, Steve will be there to help."

"I don't like this."

"Trust me," I said. "I can handle it."

She bit her lip as tears welled in her eyes. "I know you can. Just, please be careful, all right?"

"You know I will."

"I mean it," she said, grabbing my hand. "I don't want to lose you."

As I stared into her eyes, my fear melted away. Her gaze was so warm, her touch soft. I didn't ever want to leave her, but I knew I had to.

"I'll see you later," I said.

"You promise?"

"Promise."

I had no way of guaranteeing that, but I had to move fast. After giving her one last grin, I made my way down Edgar's driveway and began wracking my brain for the fastest way to get to Mick's. I figured I could probably run most of it and cut through yards to save on time. The moon was already full, but I remembered the last time Mick had changed, it had taken a while for the magic to take effect. Then again, I had no real idea how any of it worked. For all I knew, he could've already changed and was wreaking havoc all over town. I was just rounding the corner to Edgar's driveway when I saw Aunt Joy rushing from her house. She pulled her cardigan tight across her shoulders while looking to the fire with a terrified expression. It was then that it hit me. Aunt Joy had a car. Cars moved fast. Before she could speak, I stepped in front of her and held up my hands.

"I need a ride," I said quickly.

"A *ride?*"

"Yeah, to Mick's place."

"Charlie, what in god's name is going on here?"

"We need to hurry. I promise I'll explain everything in the car."

Her eyebrow raised. "Or how about you explain right *now*. Edgar's house is on fire for crying out loud."

"Just trust me," I said. "This is an emergency."

She furrowed her brow and looked from me to the fire. After a moment, she finally let out a breath.

"Fine," she said. "Just let me grab my keys."

"Thank you."

I let out a sigh of relief, and before I knew it, she was back with her car keys in hand. I hopped right in and slammed the door shut. It wasn't until we pulled out of the driveway, and I heard the distant sounds of sirens that I started to feel better. Whether that was the ambulance or a fire truck, I knew it meant Andy and Scotty would be okay. I told myself that over and over until I started to believe it. They would be okay; they just had to be.

"All right," Aunt Joy said, "You got about five minutes until we get to Mick's, so you better start explaining now."

"Right."

I turned the tranquilizer dart over in my hands and wondered where the hell to even start; there just wasn't enough time to cover it all. I decided to start from the top and told her about my powers as well as the basics on Edgar and what was going on around town. I was talking so fast, and all the while she remained silent. God, she probably thought I was totally warped, but a promise was a promise, and I said I'd tell her the truth, so I kept talking and talking until I was blue in the face. By the time I got around to breaking the news about Mick and his being a werewolf, we were almost to his place.

"I'm sorry," I said. "I should've told you sooner. I guess I just didn't want you to freak out."

For the first time, I looked at her and was surprised to see she appeared relatively. In fact, she was laughing.

"What's so funny?" I asked.

"You know, my sister was married to your father, right?'

"Yeah, so?"

"So, Nadine and I were close. You don't think she mentioned your father's powers once or twice?"

My jaw dropped.

"Oh, honey," she said, patting my leg. "I know what a Venator is. I've known this whole time."

"Why didn't you say anything?"

"Because you were already so shy and timid, especially when it came to your father. I didn't want to make you uncomfortable. Besides, I knew you'd come to me when you were ready."

I stared at her, my mouth gaping. After all this time, she knew. She *knew*. I just couldn't wrap my head around it. When the shock finally wore off, I realized she was right. When I first moved in with her, the last thing I wanted was to talk about my father or any of that supernatural bull crap. In that moment, I was more than grateful that she'd let me come to her in my own time. Granted, it took a house burning down, and my best friend morphing into a werewolf to get me there, but all the same, I was so damn thankful to have her. I loved her. God, I *loved* her. I wanted to finally say it right then and there, but the car came to a screeching halt in front of Mick's place.

I had to focus.

When I stepped outside, the crisp night air blew through my hair and sent chills down my spine. The crickets were chirping, the street lights were one, and all was too quiet for there being a werewolf on the loose. Mick's house seemed eerie to me. It was probably because I knew what horrors awaited me beyond that front door.

I'd hardly started up Mick's driveway when I heard footsteps pounding on the inside of his house. My heart leapt from my chest, and I stopped in my tracks. The next thing I knew, the front door burst open. It was Steve, his face as pale as a sheet of paper as he slammed the door shut and fell against it. Aunt Joy and I rushed over, and as soon as he saw us he stood straight and pushed his sweaty hair from his face.

"Where the hell were you?" he asked.

"It's a long story, but I'm here now," I said.

"What about Andy?"

"She's fine, but I'll fill you in on that later," I said. "Where's Mick?"

"Inside."

"Has he…?"

"Fuck yeah," he said. "After it got dark, and the moon came out, we started to panic. We did everything we could to try and lock him in the basement, but it's only a matter of time before he—"

There was a loud crash from inside.

I closed my eyes as a grim realization came over me. "Please tell me Mick's mom isn't in there."

Steve gulped. "She's in her room."

I cursed under my breath and tightened my grip on the dart. "Well then, I guess we better hurry."

"Where's the gun?" he asked.

"We lost it," I said.

"You *what*?"

"Don't worry," I said. "I still have the dart. We'll just have to distract Mick so I can get close enough to use it."

"Distract a *werewolf*?" he exclaimed.

"We don't have much choice." I turned to Aunt Joy. "I'm gonna need you to go upstairs. Mick's mom's room is the first on the right. Lock yourself in with her and barricade it with anything you can find."

She nodded.

I turned to Steve. "You and me are gonna find Mick. Stay close; once we know where he is, we'll just figure it out from there."

"So, we're winging it then?" he asked.

"It's the best we got," I said.

As I turned to face the front door, a daunting feeling came over me. It seemed like an eternity had passed before I was able to muster up the courage to push open the door. As I did, it creaked, a loud, unnerving sound that felt like a very clear warning to turn back. Run away. Danger ahead. But I pushed those thoughts from my mind and forced myself to step inside. It wasn't until Aunt Joy made her way up the stairs that I started to feel a tiny bit better; at least she'd be safe. I couldn't really say the same for Steve and me. It felt as though we were marching to certain death.

We continued down the long hallway that led to the kitchen. I couldn't help but think it was strangely quiet for a house that was plagued by a rogue werewolf. Something was definitely off. The only thing that gave me peace of mind was the fact that there were no open doors or broken windows; that meant he had to be somewhere inside.

It was then that I spotted the basement door. It was closed, though it was dented right in the middle with little splinters of wood sprinkled on the floor as if someone had been trying to get out. I nudged Steve and motioned for him to follow me toward it.

When I reached for the doorknob, a strange feeling started to brew in the pit of my stomach. I couldn't really explain it, but it was the same feeling as before where I just knew something wasn't right. The premonition was screaming at me as I opened the door and found the lights in the basement dimmed. There were no sounds. Nothing out of the ordinary, just the usual old *Misfits* band poster framed at the very bottom of the steps. Steve pointed to it and lowered his voice.

"Before he changed, we handcuffed him to the wall," he said. "Maybe he's still down there."

"Maybe," I said.

Just then, there was a low growl, only it wasn't coming from the basement—it was coming from behind us. I held my breath as Steve grabbed my arm, his hands shaking as we slowly turned to meet our fate. Sure enough, standing with only a kitchen island between us was Mick.

He was just as I remembered him, seven-feet-tall with ginormous, rippling muscles and terrifying, sharp fangs. His yellow eyes were locked on us and wrapped in his mondo paws was something metal. Before I could figure out just what it was, a frying pan was soaring through the air. Without thinking, I ducked. Steve on the other hand wasn't as lucky. The frying pan hit him square in the chest and he went tumbling down the staircase. I watched in horror as his body bent and twisted with each step he hit, until finally he reached the bottom. He sprawled out and began groaning under his breath, but at least he was alive. I wasted no time and slammed the door shut before sprinting off.

I was thankful when I heard Mick blow right past the basement door and chase after me, though at the same time *he was chasing after me.* I was running on adrenaline with no idea what I was going to do or where I was going. I just ran. I made a break for the garage and was almost able to shut the door behind me, but right before I could, Mick collided with it. I was no match for a fully grown werewolf and went soaring backwards, landing on the hard, concrete floor. The tranquilizer dart slipped from my hands, as a sharp pain shot through my shoulder. I heard it clatter and roll under the small, white Toyota parked next to me. Cursing under my breath, I crawled on my forearms as fast as I could to try to retrieve it. It was lying in an oil puddle, the pink feather tip just out of reach. I was so close, barely an inch away when I felt a burning pain in my leg.

I screamed and glanced over my shoulder to find Mick with his claws dug into my calf. He growled and tightened his grip, blood now staining my jeans. The pain was so intense, I was starting to black out, but I forced myself to stay present. He tugged me back, and I looked to the dart which was growing smaller in the distance. I began to imagine how it'd feel for my muscles to be torn to pieces, my face clawed to shreds, but then, to my surprise, Mick loosened his grip. I scrunched my brow in confusion and turned around, only to find Aunt Joy with a baseball bat cocked on her shoulder.

Mick stared her down, and she got ready to swing, but before she could, he swiped her across the face. The bat clattered to the ground, and she collapsed like a rag doll. Before I could do anything, Mick pounced on top of her.

I pushed through the pain and lunged for the dart. After grabbing it, I shot to my feet and threw my whole body at Mick, plunging the dart straight into his neck. He knocked me with his elbow, sending me right back to the ground. I braced myself, but instead of getting mauled, I opened my eyes to find Mick stumbling around in a daze, his eyelids fluttering before he fell next to me with a thud.

He passed out.

I did it.

It was *over*.

But I didn't care. I hardly even had time to think about that because the only thing on my mind was my aunt.

I rushed to her side, my heart hammering in my chest. She wasn't moving, and from what I could tell, she was hardly breathing. And there was so much blood; it was smeared all over her face and shirt to the point where I couldn't even tell where it was coming from. I swore under my breath and cradled her head.

"Please wake up," I whimpered. "Please, please wake up."

She didn't move.

I raised my voice. "*Please.*"

Nothing.

I buried my face in her chest. "You can't do this. I need you. I *need* you!"

There were footsteps, and then Steve was at my side. He already had a nasty bruise on his face and was clutching at his chest where the pan had hit. When he saw my aunt, he stood straight.

"Oh, shit," he said.

"Call an ambulance," I demanded.

"But what about Mick?"

"I don't care," I snapped. "Just call an ambulance right fucking *now*. We'll figure it out later."

I turned back to Aunt Joy, my eyes filled with tears. Her skin was losing color fast, and her breaths were growing weaker. I caressed her face, not caring about my clothes which were now soaked in her blood.

"I love you," I whispered.

I needed her to know that. She was everything to me. The most important person in my life. *I loved her*. I repeated it over and over until I broke into uncontrollable sobs; I just hoped I wasn't too late.

Steve had to physically tear me from my aunt's side so we could move her outside and close the garage door behind us to hide Mick's body. Before I knew it, the night was shining with red and blue lights; the paramedics were swarming us. I was in a total daze as Steve fed them a bullshit story about how we'd been on a walk when some stray wolf attacked us. The entire time he spoke, I couldn't look away from my aunt, especially as they laid her on the stretcher and loaded her into the back of the ambulance.

The next thing I knew, we were at the hospital, and Aunt Joy was being rushed down a narrow hallway. I desperately wanted to go after her, but they wouldn't let me. Instead, they began plaguing me with question after question about my leg. I must've been running on pure adrenaline, because up until that point, I had barely felt anything. When I finally looked down, I was surprised to find my jeans were torn to shreds and there was a bloody gash in my calf. Just then, a rush of dizziness took over, and I stumbled back, catching myself on Steve's arm.

There was fog and blurriness and the next thing I knew, I was sitting on a hospital bed, and a nurse was cleaning my wound. She offered me some sleeping pills which I took because truth be told, I was so damn anxious. I figured they'd at least help take off the edge. They worked a bit better than I'd anticipated, and the second I put my head on the pillow, I was out like a light.

That sleep was everything. It was such a deep sleep, I didn't dream. I didn't even *exist*. I simply took a break from living for a short bit. When I eventually woke, the sun was already shining high in the sky and birds were chirping outside my window. It was a total reset.

But then I blinked a few times as memories from the night before came hurtling at me like a freight train. Back to reality.

It was then that I noticed Steve in the chair next to me, and I sat up. He wore a green flannel, which was unbuttoned low enough to expose a thick, white bandage over his chest. His leg was wrapped in a cast, and leaning against the wall next to him was a pair of crutches. When he noticed I was awake, he lowered the magazine he'd been reading and grinned.

"Morning, sleepyhead," he said.

"What time is it?" I asked in a groggy voice.

"Almost noon, dude," he said. "You were passed the hell out, snoring and shit. Mick's chilling over in Scotty and Andy's room, so I figured I'd keep your ass company until you woke up."

"Are they okay?"

"Yeah, they're fine," he said, adding after a brief pause, "for the most part."

"What's that mean?"

"Scotty," he said, his smile fading. "He's alive and all, but they couldn't save his hand."

"Oh…"

"Yeah, it's the pits," he muttered. "I mean; he seems okay for the most part. Like, he's the same ol' dude, bossing everyone around and shit, but you can sort of tell that it's really buggin' him."

"Right," I mumbled.

"He'll be okay," he added quickly. "It's Scotty; he can handle it."

I rubbed my hands over my face and let out a deep sigh. This was my fault. All my fault. I reminded myself how none of us would even be here if it weren't for me. My mind flashed to Aunt Joy, and a sick feeling turned my stomach. I was almost too afraid to ask, but I eventually forced the words out.

"How is she?" I asked softly.

"Not sure," he said. "The last I heard, the doctors said she'd lost a lot of blood, but other than that, they're not giving me straight answers. And believe me, I've been hounding those assholes all morning."

I nodded, though it was hard to hide the tears welling in my eyes. He placed a hand on my shoulder as I blinked them away and tried to convince myself that she'd be okay. She had to be. The doctors just didn't want to make any promises, that was all. I finally gathered myself and looked at Steve.

"Can we go see the others?" I asked.

"Sure can," he said. "They're just down the hall."

I didn't realize just how much my leg had hurt until I tried to stand on it for the first time. It felt like my muscles had been ripped from my body and thrown into a blender. When I finally got a grip on the pain, Steve and I hobbled down the hall like two war vets who'd just returned from battle. As soon as I walked into Andy and Scotty's room, I took a look around. It was much like my room, simple and white. The only difference was it was a bit larger with more furniture and a TV that hung from the ceiling. Andy and Mick were on one bed playing a game of cards while Scotty sat bolt upright on the other bed, his eyes glued to the news. I felt a hitch in my stomach when I noticed the way his arm was cradled in his lap. It tapered off near his wrist and was bandaged with white gauze.

"Come sit," he said, never taking his eyes from the television. "We have a lot to talk about."

"What do you mean?" I asked.

"Have you been watching the news?"

"No," I said.

"Well, I have," he replied. "Last night, a crater appeared seemingly out of nowhere in the middle of a busy road just outside of Las Vegas. So far, it's been recorded at twenty feet in diameter, but oddly enough, they have no clue on its depth. As far as they can tell, it goes on forever."

"So what?" I asked.

"Yeah," Andy said. "That's all the way out in Vegas. What's it got to do with us?"

"Well," he said, "they're saying it appeared right around the time that Edgar broke the final seal. I can't be completely certain that this has to do with the horsemen, but it's a great lead. And I don't know about you guys, but as soon as they release me from the hospital, I'm packing up my trailer and heading west."

"I'm going with you," I said, the words taking me by surprise. But the more I thought about it, the more it started to make sense. This was my mess, so it had to be me that cleaned it up.

"Great," Scotty said. "I could really use a Venator's help."

"I'm going, too," Mick piped up.

"Yeah, count me in," Andy said.

"Same," Steve added. "I've always wanted to tear up Sin City."

"This isn't a vacation," Scotty said. "The horsemen are no joke. Everything thus far has been child's play compared to this."

"Whatever," Steve said.

"Yeah," Mick added. "We're still going."

"No you're not," I cut in. "Scotty's right; this is dangerous."

Mick furrowed his brow. "You don't want us with you?"

I shook my head. "It's not that."

"Then what is it?" he asked.

"Scotty's right; this is too dangerous," I said. "We'll manage on our own.”

“Yeah, but—”

“Don’t you get it?” I snapped. “You guys are in the hospital right now because of me. None of this had to happen. You guys could have normal lives. You could finish high school, maybe even go to college.”

“So can you,” he said.

“No,” I replied. “This is what I was born to do. I can’t just ignore it. And I’ve already put you guys in enough danger as it is; you’re not risking your lives for me anymore. This isn’t your fight.”

Mick opened his mouth to argue, but closed it suddenly. There was pain behind his eyes, something I hated to see, but I had no choice. I couldn’t put my friends in any more danger. Before either of us could say a word, the door opened and a nurse walked in. When she saw me, her eyes widened.

“There you are,” she said. “I’ve been looking everywhere for you.”

“What is it?” I asked.

“Your aunt,” she said. “She’s awake.”

Her words were like a punch to the gut and suddenly, the horsemen faded to the back of my mind. All that mattered was that my aunt was awake. Without wasting another second, I rushed out of the room and followed the nurse. The walk felt like an eternity, and with each step, my chest grew tighter until I couldn’t breathe. It got worse once we finally stopped in front of what I presumed to be Aunt Joy’s room.

The nurse was saying something or another, but I couldn’t hear her. All I could focus on was whether or not my aunt was okay. When the door finally opened, my heart leapt from my chest. There she was, lying in her hospital bed. For the longest time, I remained frozen in place. It was her, but at the same time it wasn’t. She had no makeup on, something I’d never seen before, and her auburn hair was a tangled nest atop her head. There were tubes in her nose and an IV bag hanging over her head. From what I could see, she had nasty bruises and cuts along her neck and arms, but the hardest thing to stomach was the deep slash that went from the top of her forehead, right across her face and down to her chin. I must've been staring for a long time because eventually, she let out a soft laugh.

"Oh, Charlie," she said. "Quit staring at me like a dead woman, and come give me a hug."

It was as if everything hit me all at once, and I ran to her. The second I was close enough, I threw my arms around her and buried my face into her shoulder. When we finally parted, she used her thumb to wipe the tears in my eye. I hadn't even realized I'd been crying, but suddenly, I couldn't stop.

"I love you," I choked out through sobs. "I love you so much. I'm sorry I didn't say it sooner."

"I love you too," she said.

"I thought..." I closed my eyes and swallowed. "I thought I lost you."

"Well, you didn't," she said. "I'm right here."

There was a moment of silence as I studied the cut across her face. Now that I was close enough to get a better look, I could see just how deep it was with little black stitches sewn into her skin.

"Your face," I whispered.

"Oh, please," she said. "I'm a drag queen, honey. Gimme a bottle of Lancome's foundation and consider it as good as new."

I let out a weak laugh and shook my head. She was always so good at getting me to smile, even when I thought it was impossible. I had no clue what I was going to do without her once I left for Vegas.

Vegas.

For the first time, it really hit me. I was leaving. A bittersweet sorrow washed over me, and I looked to my shoes. I'd only just gotten her back, and already I was going to have to say goodbye.

"I can't stay with you anymore," I said suddenly.

"Why not?"

"This whole thing with Edgar… it's bigger than I thought, and it's up to me to make it right."

I pushed my hair from my face and began to wonder how the hell I would fully explain all that was going on. All that I'd have to *do*. How I was leaving her to pursue the life of a damn vagabond. But before I could figure out the right words to say, she grabbed my hand.

"I understand," she said.

"Huh?"

"Oh, honey," she said. "I'm sure you're going to hate hearing this, but you sound just like your father right now. He was a Venator through and through, always going on about how it was his destiny to travel the world and rid us all from evil. It just simply wasn't in his blood to stay in one place for more than a few months' time. He was a noble man, and I respected him for that, but here's the thing—destiny is bullshit. That's the beauty of life, Charlie. We can choose our own path. Now, I don't exactly know what's going on, or why you can't stay in Midtowne, but just know, you don't have to carry the weight of the world on your shoulders. This is your life, and no one else's."

I looked to my lap as her words fully resonated with me. She was right; it was completely my choice. I could choose to live a normal life. I could choose to stay in Midtowne with my friends, with *her*. But as tempting as that sounded, something about it just didn't feel right. As much as I hated to admit it, that life just wasn't for me.

"I have to go," I said softly.

"Charlie..."

"This is what I want," I continued. "Don't get me wrong, these past few months living in Midtowne with you have been amazing, but I don't belong here. My whole life, I've been an outcast. There was just always something so different about me. I couldn't really figure it out until I learned about my heritage. And I don't know. It's hard to explain, but I guess ever since then, it just sort of feels right."

"Are you sure?"

"I am."

She stared at me longingly until finally, a smile appeared on her face. "Well, okay then. If that's what you want, then I support you."

"You do?"

"Of course, Charlie. You're my nephew. I love you"

I wrapped my arms around her once more, and though it was hard, I forced myself to let her go. Leaving her was going to be almost impossible, but it was without a doubt the right thing to do.

"I love you," I said.

"Oh, honey..." She brushed the hair from my eyes and grinned. "I love you, too. I'll always love you. Just know that wherever life takes you, you'll always have a home with your Aunt Joy."

I adjusted the duffel bag on my shoulder as I walked past the wrought iron gate and down the gravel path of Scotty's trailer park. It was just as I had remembered it, though this time around it was daylight, so there were no ominous street lamps, and the place didn't look like a total ghost town. His trailer was parked beneath the same willow tree a before and had the same dismal slate gray exterior with bright red hieroglyphics painted on the siding, complete with a wooden crucifix fence.

I noticed Scotty hunched over the bumper of his truck with his teeth gritted in frustration. His hair was sweaty and tied back beneath his trademark red bandanna, and his stump was covered by a thick, white bandage. As I walked closer, he cursed at the top of his lungs and kicked the bumper in frustration. I dropped my bag to my side, and he spun around. When he realized it was me, he straightened.

"Oh, Charlie," he said. "I didn't see you there."

"Need some help?" I asked.

"No."

"You sure? I could—"

"Yes, I'm *sure*," he said, his tone sharp. "I think I know how to hitch my own trailer, thank you very much. I've done it a million times before, and I can do it again without your help."

"Sorry," I said, holding up my hands.

He shot me a dirty look before returning his attention to the hitch. I watched awkwardly as he struggled to connect the two, all while grunting and griping under his breath. As much as I wanted to step in and do something, I knew it'd piss him off even more, so I just kept my mouth shut until he eventually figured it out himself. With a proud smile, he stood tall and nodded at his work.

"See?" he said. "Told you I could do it."

"Nice job," I muttered.

He snatched my bag and threw it in the back seat. "So according to the plans I have set out, the drive shouldn't take more than a few days so long as things go smoothly and we limit our stops."

"Sounds good," I said.

"I already packed my stuff in my trailer, so that should be it." He leaned against his truck and looked at me. "So, are you ready?"

"Mmhmm."

"That doesn't sound very convincing."

"I'm ready," I said, forcing a smile. "Promise."

"If you say so." He opened the driver's side door and grinned. "All right then, let's hit the road."

He climbed into his truck and shut the door behind him. As I walked around to the passenger's side, I felt a hint of nerves in my gut. It all just started to feel so real—I was actually leaving Midtowne, and I wasn't exactly sure how to feel about that. I mean, on the one hand, I've only been here for a few months. But at the same time, this was the closest thing I've ever had to a home. With my hand lingering on the door handle, I took a deep breath, and that's when I heard it.

Music.

It was distant at first, but grew louder with each passing second until I whipped around to find a ginormous Winnebago barreling right toward me. It was dirty and white with a yellow and orange stripe that cut right through the middle. I gasped as it came to a screeching halt, sending a cloud of dust and dirt into the air. As I coughed and waved my hand in front of my face the radio cut and the door kicked open, and suddenly, there was Mick. Andy followed right behind, and then Steve came rushing around from the driver's side. I scrunched my brow in confusion as they gathered around me, smiling. Before I could say anything, Steve slapped the side of the van.

"This here's the 1976 Chieftain Turbo LS Winnebago," he said. "My family used to take it camping, but it's been years since we've stepped foot in the woods, so they shouldn't notice I swiped it."

"What do you mean you swiped it?" I asked.

"For our trip to Vegas, dummy."

My mouth fell open, and I immediately shook my head. "I already told you guys, there's no way you're going."

"Oh, come *on*," Steve groaned.

"No," I stated firmly.

Mick rolled his eyes. "Would you just give it up already? It's not like we need your permission."

"Yeah, but—"

"You're wasting your time," Andy said. "We're coming with you whether you like it or not."

"Admit it, dude," Steve added. "You'd be dead without us. I mean, think about it. Before we were in your life, you were a total worm, and now look at you. You're a great, big, beautiful butterfly."

Andy raised her eyebrow. "Worms don't turn into butterflies, dumbass."

"They don't?" he asked.

"No," she said. "That's caterpillars."

"Whatever," he said. "I'm sure he gets the point."

"Guys…" I pinched the bridge of my nose and sighed. "You're not risking your lives for me."

"Whoa there, Charlie, man," Mick said. "The world's in danger, and you think we're risking our lives for *your* sorry ass?" He nudged Steve with his elbow and smirked. "Can you believe this guy?"

"What a selfish prick," Steve said.

"This is serious," I said.

"Yeah, I know," Mick replied. "And I'm pretty damn serious when I say we're going to Vegas with or without you, man. You ain't stoppin' us. We talked it over, and this is what we want to do."

"We already made up our minds," Steve said.

"Yeah," Andy added. "Now, you can try to fight us, or you can just shut up and get in the damn van."

I pressed my lips together and looked to my shoes. It felt like no matter what I said, they just weren't hearing me. The crazy thing was, I really wanted them to come with. Of course I did, but I was terrified. I just wouldn't be able to live with myself if something happened to one of them. But Mick was right; they didn't need my permission. And the more I thought about it, the more I realized there was really nothing I could do. After a moment, I looked up from my shoes with a smile.

"It's your funeral," I said.

"So, is that a yes?" Mick asked.

I shrugged. "You said it yourself; you don't need my permission."

He grinned. "You bet your ass we don't."

Scotty checked his watch and scoffed. "Can we get a move on? I'd like to make it to Vegas sometime this decade."

"You heard the man," Mick said. "Sin City, here we come!"

"Hell yeah!" Steve shouted.

"Great," Scotty mumbled as he climbed back in his truck. "Las Vegas with Scooby and the gang, just what I always wanted."

As my friends cheered and piled into the Winnebago, I stayed put and took a moment to really process everything. If a few months ago you were to tell me I'd be going to Vegas with my friends to stop some mythical force from destroying the world, I would've called you crazy. Hell, I would've called you crazy if you just told me I'd have *friends*. The truth was, I spent my whole life in hiding. I hid from my father. I hid from my powers. God, I hid from just about anything at all that . scared me. I was watching life from the bleachers, never really joining in. But not anymore. Now, I was confident. I was brave. I had people in my life who I loved; people worth fighting for. With my friends by my side, I felt invincible.

As I stood before that huge Winnebago with the yellow and orange stripe, I made a promise to myself to never hide again.

Never.

From now on, I was on the hunt.